What Teens Are Saying About
DIARY OF A TEENAGE GIRL SERIES...

"Your books are so captivating. I feel like my life is being lived out in those pages. I think that's what I love about them. No other series could teach me about life the way your books do."—CATHÉRINE

"I LOVE your books!!! I've just finished *Face the Music,* and it wuz awesome! I couldn't put it down. I've loaned all my books of the Chloe series to my friends, and they love them too!"—ALLISON

"Your books are so awesome! I started reading them, then one of my unsaved friends decided to borrow them, and now she's saved. I have you and God to thank for that! Your books are really powerful. I love them."—LYNETTE

"I love the characters in your Diary series. I am about to start my freshman year of college and loved *On My Own.* I feel like Caitlin is one of my own friends."—HEATHER

"It is amazing to me how you write with such insight, as if you really are living in a modern-day world for teens. Thank you!"—DEEDEE

"I love reading your books! I found myself in a whole different world. Like someone had shown me a different part of me."
—SARAH

"You have helped me in so many ways. Just reading your books brought me closer to God. Caitlin is the best friend i wish i had."
—MELISSA

"Your writing inspires me. You truly have a gift."—JENNIFER

"I LOVE the way that you write. God has certainly blessed you with an amazing talent for writing and understanding people. I will probably continue to buy and read your books when I'm forty."—HJK

DIARY OF A TEENAGE GIRL

CAITLIN BOOK Nº. 5

I DO!

A NOVEL

MELODY CARLSON

Multnomah Books

YA Carls

I DO!
published by Multnomah Books
in association with the literary agency of Sara A. Fortenberry

© 2004 by Carlson Management Co., Inc.
International Standard Book Number: 978-1-59052-320-9

Cover design by David Carlson Design
Cover photo by Jeremy Samuelson/Getty Images

Scripture quotations are from:
The Holy Bible, New International Version © 1973, 1984 by International Bible Society,
used by permission of Zondervan Publishing House

Published in the United States by WaterBrook Multnomah, an imprint of the Crown
Publishing Group, a division of Random House Inc., New York.

MULTNOMAH and its mountain colophon are registered trademarks of Random House Inc.

Printed in the United States of America

For information:
MULTNOMAH BOOKS
12265 ORACLE BOULEVARD, SUITE 200 • COLORADO SPRINGS, CO 80921

Library of Congress Cataloging-in-Publication Data
Carlson, Melody.
    I do! : a novel / Melody Carlson.
        p. cm. — (Diary of a teenage girl. Caitlin ; bk. 5)
    Summary: Twenty-one-year-old Caitlin starts a new diary to record her experiences when
she becomes engaged and has to struggle to remember to focus on God, her friends, and
her senior year in college as her head swims with wedding plans.

    ISBN 1-59052-320-2
    [1. Weddings—Fiction. 2. Christian life—Fiction. 3. Interpersonal relations—Fiction.
4. Colleges and universities—Fiction. 5. Diaries—Fiction.]   I Title.

PZ7.C216637Id 2004
[Fic]—dc22

                                2004019846

                        10—10 9 8 7

BOOKS BY MELODY CARLSON:

Piercing Proverbs

DIARY OF A TEENAGE GIRL SERIES

Caitlin O'Conner:

Becoming Me

It's My Life

Who I Am

On My Own

I Do!

Chloe Miller:

My Name Is Chloe

Sold Out

Road Trip

Face the Music

Kim Peterson:

Just Ask

Meant to Be

TRUE COLOR SERIES

Dark Blue, color me lonely

Deep Green, color me jealous

Torch Red, color me torn

Pitch Black, color me lost

Burnt Orange, color me wasted

ONE

Saturday, October 22

My life changed today. It's as if I got up this morning as one person and will go to bed as someone else. Okay, maybe it's not as drastic as all that. But believe me, things are definitely different now. Excitingly different even. I'm not sure that I'll ever be able to go to sleep tonight. And ironically, here I am in my old bedroom in my parents' home, the very same place I was when I began writing in my very first diary almost five years ago.

And as a result of what happened today, I think it's time to break out a brand-new diary. Okay, this one isn't exactly "brand-new," since it's actually one that I've been saving for quite a while. It's a rather ordinary looking diary (really, more like a journal), but my friend Josh Miller gave it to me on my nineteenth birthday, just a couple of years ago. I thought it was sweet of him at the time, but I was also right in the middle of writing in another diary, so I tucked this special leather-bound book into my top bureau drawer—to save for another time.

Another time has come, and that time is now because:

Josh Miller asked me to marry him tonight!

Okay, okay, let's start back at the beginning of this incredibly romantic day. I'd come home from college this weekend to attend a wedding. Two friends of mine were getting hitched—Willy Johnson (the manager of the incredible rock band Redemption) and Elise Curtis (mother of Redemption drummer Allie Curtis). I replaced Elise, last summer, when I traveled as a chaperone for Redemption. And as a result, these three gifted girls feel like family to me. Especially Chloe Miller, who will become my sister-in-law sometime next year. Wow, it's still sinking in! God is so amazing!

The Johnson-Curtis wedding was absolutely beautiful. Oh, it was nothing lavish or fancy or over the top. And only about a hundred guests were there. But the ceremony felt very real to me, and the love between Willy and Elise was written all over their happy faces. I actually cried—it was that sweet.

Chloe, Allie, and Laura were bridesmaids, all wearing the most gorgeous gowns designed by none other than my old best friend Beanie Jacobs. The dresses were autumnal colors with lots of beadwork and lace, but not a bit frilly. Just really elegant and classy and like something you'd see in a movie. Beanie's majoring in textile design now and is rumored to have the kind of talent that will take her places. I'm so proud of her!

All right, I will admit that I had a brief fantasy during this particular wedding ceremony. I mean, what girl doesn't dream about her own wedding day? Especially when you hear those familiar notes of "The Wedding March" starting to play! <u>Dum, dum, da-dum.</u> I'm sure I've been humming that tune since I was a little girl putting my mom's old white negligee over my head like a wedding veil. And okay, I did wonder how I would feel to be the one standing up there in a scrumptious white gown and repeating my vows to...well, I even had a particular guy in mind.

In fact, that guy was actually one of the groomsmen standing up there with Willy and looking totally awesome in his dark brown rented tux with velvet lapels. It was in that exact same moment that I realized Josh was actually staring back at me. It seemed as if our eyes locked for about five minutes, although I'm sure it was only a few seconds before I looked away. Maybe that's what made me cry.

I suppose I was sort of embarrassed to be caught gaping at the same guy I have consistently pushed away over the years. It's hard to believe that it all started back in high school, when he was a senior and I was a junior. But then our relationship went sideways, and it was time to break up.

Oh, we're friends now. And better friends than we've

ever been before. We've even had a few talks that
made me wonder...but then I always remember how
many times I made it perfectly clear to Josh (especially
back during my first year of college when he says I
broke his heart) that I couldn't be serious with him.

Not that I wouldn't have liked being serious with Josh.
I mean, all you have to do is to read my other diaries to
know that this guy totally gets to me. Believe me, there's
always been a strong attraction to that boy. But even
so, I knew that I had to keep him at a safe distance.
Let's just say that it was a God-thing. Because I'd committed myself to abstaining from sex until marriage, and
as a result, gave up dating in general. So there was no
room in my life for Josh as a boyfriend. Consequently, I
think I've really learned about priorities these past few
years. God is always first, family and friends next, and
then school (since that's sort of my "job" at the moment).
And that's a full load. Getting serious with a guy just did
not fit into that picture.

Even so, I never stopped loving Josh. And there have
been times (like dozens!) when I was so scared that Josh
would forget all about me and just write me off and
marry someone else. I mean, there had to be hundreds
of girls out there who knew what a catch this guy was.
Not only is Josh cute (have I mentioned he looks like Matt
Damon?) with blue eyes and the greatest smile ever, but
he loves God with his whole heart, and he's the most honest and sincere guy I know. But enough about that for
now—since I can feel my pulse rate increasing!

Anyway, each time I'd start to freak over the possibility of another girl snatching up the guy I loved, I tried
really hard to give this fear to God. And it wasn't
always easy. But it usually boiled down to trust. I knew I
needed to trust God completely. I had to believe that
my life and my future (as well as Josh's) were in His
hands. That was my lifeline.

Back to today's wedding. Following the ceremony, we
all traipsed down the stairs for a fairly no-frills reception
in the church basement, which is nothing to write home
about. I mean, our church is about as plain and boring as
they come. It's in an old department store building downtown, but due to recent remodeling, the "sanctuary" is
fairly spacious and the basement (which still smells like
cardboard) actually has pretty good acoustics. That
came in handy since Redemption played a few songs for
the wedding guests. Just a few quiet numbers that
made both Willy and Elise teary eyed.

I was slightly surprised that there were no decorations—no ribbons or candles and very few flowers. But
Chloe informed me that Willy and Elise wanted to keep
everything as simple as possible. "It's supposed to be low-
key," she said, as if she knew I had noticed that the
room looked somewhat Spartan. Not that you need hundreds of roses or miles of satin ribbons and greenery, but
I suppose that most of the weddings I've gone to have
been pretty elaborate affairs—not to mention quite
expensive.

"Yeah," Allie said in a hushed voice. "Believe it or not,

the cake is from the grocery store bakery where my mom used to work."

"It looks nice," I said. Okay, it was a bit boring, and I suspected it wouldn't be too tasty. But it had the traditional three tiers with the little plastic bride and groom on top. And when Willy and Elise sliced into it, I'm sure it didn't matter to them whether it came from Albertsons down the street or the finest French bakery in Manhattan.

And it didn't matter to me either. Mostly I just enjoyed visiting with my church friends and a few old high school buddies, and finally congratulating Willy and Elise.

"I'm so happy for you two," I told them as we hugged.

Elise was absolutely glowing. "We are too." Then she frowned slightly. "I hope you don't feel bad that this means Davie and I will be going back on the road again." She held up her wedding ring finger. "Now that we're no longer scandal material."

Willy laughed. "Yeah, I'll bet some people think that this is just a marriage of convenience so that we can have Elise back as the chaperone again."

Elise leaned over and kissed her groom on the cheek. "Let them think what they like."

"Not that you weren't a great chaperone, Caitlin" Willy said, as if he suddenly remembered that I was still standing there. "You know you'll always be welcome."

I laughed. "Don't worry, you two. I had to give up the chaperone gig for now anyway. My plate's pretty full with my senior year."

"Still doing the double major?" Willy asked with a slightly concerned look.

I nodded. "Yeah. I like the pressure."

"What are you taking?" asked Elise.

"It's kind of an odd combo. Journalism and child development."

Willy smiled. "Well, if you graduate and end up jobless, I'm sure that the girls would welcome you back as their chaperone by next summer."

"You can say that again," Allie said with a mischievous grin. Of course, knowing Allie, I'm sure she'd prefer having me to her mom. Not that she likes me more than her mom, but she probably thinks she can get away with more stuff with me. Not that I ever let her. If anything, I think I was pretty strict with those girls.

Then just as Beanie and I were about to leave the reception, Josh stopped me. He and I already had one very brief conversation that had been interrupted by the photographer wanting to get some group shots of the wedding party.

"Don't leave yet," he said to me as he waved to someone calling his name from across the room. "I want to ask you something first."

I smiled at him. "What's that?"

"Are you busy tonight?"

I shrugged and glanced at Beanie. I'd already asked her to do something tonight, but she'd informed me that she needed to spend some time with her mom. "Not really," I said to Josh. "Why?"

"Do you think you could grab a bite with me?" He smiled in that cute but sly way of his (like he's keeping something from me). "You know, just two old friends catching up?"

"Of course," I told him. "I'd love to."

So he said he'd pick me up at six.

"You guys have a good time tonight," Beanie said when I dropped her off at her mom's place. Since Beanie's dad left when she was a baby, it's so cool that her mom finally found and married a great guy. And they have a house that's so much nicer than where they used to live. I know Beanie appreciates it when she comes home to visit.

"Thanks," I told Beanie, but something about her expression made me wonder. It's like she had this secret joke going on. Okay, maybe I realize this more in retrospect. You know, that old twenty-twenty hindsight kind of thing.

But I do think I started getting a bit suspicious when Josh picked me up. I had already changed into jeans and a sweater (okay, they were cute jeans and a nice sweater), but Josh had on a sleek-looking sports jacket and a <u>tie.</u> Josh hardly ever wears a tie.

"You didn't tell me it was formal," I said, feeling a little uncomfortable.

"You're fine, Caitlin."

I tried to suppress my feelings of being underdressed as I admired how handsome he looked. "So are you starting to dress like a pastor all the time now?"

He smiled as he navigated his Jeep Wrangler through traffic. "From what I hear, most pastors can't afford to dress too well."

"Oh, so you're making the most of it before you've forced to start digging through the missionary barrels then?"

He laughed. "I guess."

"So, how's it really going, Josh? Do you like your new job as the youth pastor? Chloe and Allie say that you're a natural."

"I pay them to say that."

I laughed. "No wonder pastors are so poor."

Then he turned more serious. "I think my parents are still a little disappointed by my career choice."

"Really? But I'd think with all that's happened with Chloe... I mean, doesn't that make them more appreciative of ministry related jobs?"

He shrugged. "Don't forget that Chloe's 'ministry' brings in the big bucks, whereas my parents are fairly sure that I've signed on for a lifetime of poverty."

I nodded. "Yeah, I guess my parents still feel like that about me too. They usually just change the subject if I mention things like wanting to go down to Mexico to work with the orphanage after I graduate."

"Same here."

After that Josh got very quiet—I mean, dead silent—and suddenly I got worried that something was troubling him. Maybe even something serious. Like was he about to tell me he only had six months to live?

Finally the silence was killing me. "Where are we going?" I asked abruptly. We'd already driven past most of the eating areas downtown.

"Someplace special."

Well, I thought this seemed a little odd, but then I don't spend much time in this town anymore. For all I knew, there might be some new restaurant out this way. But now I really wished I'd worn something nicer. I remember looking down at my feet; at least I had on a new pair of shoes. A really cute pair of Nine Wests that I'd gotten while touring with the girls last summer. It was the first time I'd worn them.

Josh pulled into a parking lot at the park, and with that same funny sort of half smile, he hopped out and opened my door, then began to lead me down one of the dirt paths. The sun was just setting, and the park was pretty soggy from an afternoon rain.

But I decided not to question this strange little escapade. I knew he was up to something, but I still had this horrible feeling that he was about to break some really bad news. As a result, I'm sure that my heart was starting to pound a little harder.

We walked a ways, and Josh managed to make small talk the whole while. I can't even remember what he said—just idle chatter about the weather and time of year kind of thing.

Suddenly we came to a clearing near the water, and it was plain to see that someone was having quite a lovely little picnic down there by the lake. The watery scene was so beautiful in the dusky blue light. The sun had just set into the trees on the other side of the lake, and there was this amazing white cloth-covered table set with china and silver and lit by a lot of softly glowing votive candles. I could even hear music playing—classical with lots of violins.

"Josh!" I whispered as I grabbed him by the arm. "We can't intrude on this. Let's turn back. It must be a party for—"

"It's for us," he said with a huge grin.

"For us?" Now I'm sure my mouth must've fallen open just then, because Josh actually started laughing at me.

He nodded. "I had this all set up for us." Then he went over to the table and pulled out a chair. "Have a seat, mademoiselle."

So we sat at this sweet, candlelit table next to the lake, and several high school-aged guys that I recognized from church began to politely serve us a lovely dinner—my favorite pesto and linguine, as well as a bunch of other delicious things. Josh confessed that someone else had done the cooking. Kind of a relief, since I'm sure I would've been intimidated to discover that he cooks better than I do.

We were both just starting to loosen up and to actually enjoy this whole crazy thing when I felt a raindrop.

Josh frowned and looked up. "We haven't even had dessert yet."

"Maybe we can get it to go."

And then it began to pour. I had a thick cotton

jacket over my sweater, but it was anything but warm and was quickly getting soaked. I didn't even want to consider my new shoes, which had gotten pretty soggy walking through the park. Then Josh hopped up from his chair, and removing his sports coat, he gently placed it over my shoulders. "Let's not go just yet."

He went down on one knee, right there on the ground that was quickly turning into a puddle, and the next thing I knew, he took my hand in his.

"Caitlin Renee O'Conner," he said, his face lit by the few candles that had survived the downpour. "I love you with all my heart. Will you do me the honor of marrying me?"

Well, I just lost it. First, I started to cry, then I threw my arms around Josh and hugged him tightly. But here's what I haven't told anyone—during this brief moment in time (a moment I will remember forever), I shot up a prayer, asking God what I was supposed to say. Then feeling certain that God was up there smiling down on us, I emphatically said, "Yes!"

Sigh... It still feels like a dream to me. Well, other than this beautiful diamond ring on my finger. That's a pretty good reminder that it's for real. It turns out that Beanie helped Josh to pick it out. She suggested I'd like a ring that was a classic style, and Josh decided on platinum. And they were both right. It's absolutely perfect, and I totally love it! Of course, Beanie was also in the loop about tonight's dinner plans. I can't believe she kept all this from me.

And finally I am so tired that I can barely keep my eyes open. I'll have to continue the ongoing saga of Josh Miller and Caitlin O'Conner tomorrow.

DEAR GOD, THANK YOU—THANK YOU—THANK YOU! THANKS FOR THIS AMAZING NIGHT! AND THANK YOU FOR FINALLY BRINGING JOSH AND ME TOGETHER LIKE THIS, ALL IN YOUR PERFECT TIMING. I'M SO GLAD THAT I WAITED ON YOU. SO GLAD THAT YOU'VE KEPT US BOTH IN YOUR HANDS. SO GLAD THAT YOU ARE TYING OUR HEARTS TOGETHER FOR ALL TIME. PRAISE YOU! THANK YOU! YOU ARE AMAZING! AMEN.

two

Sunday, October 23

I was still flying high the next morning. I got up
around eight and had coffee already brewing by the
time my parents came into the kitchen. They'd gone to
bed before I got home last night. After our damp dinner,
Josh and I went out for coffee and dessert, and of
course, we ended up talking until very late. So this morning I was preparing myself to break the big news to them.
I had no idea how they would react.

"So, what's the word, Catie?" my dad said as he
reached for his favorite coffee mug.

"Huh?" I studied his face and wondered if perhaps
he knew something about this whole thing.

"How was your, uh, your time with Josh last night?" my
mom said quickly, as if she was covering for my dad.

"Interesting..." I glanced from one to the other then
suddenly realized that they both knew something.

"What's up? What do you know about last night?"

"Well, uh, Josh came by here last week," my dad confessed.

"Why?" I watched Dad's expression.

"He just wanted to talk."

"About?"

"Come on," said my mom. "What happened last night, Caitlin? Don't keep us in suspense."

"First, you have to tell me why Josh came by here last week," I insisted.

Dad made a face like he'd just been caught. "Well, since you seem to know already...The young man wanted to ask us for your hand in marriage. There."

I suppressed a smile, still not willing to give anything away. "He did, did he?"

"Yes!" my mom exclaimed. But she was looking at me with such an imploring expression that I knew I had to tell her.

I held out my hand to show her the ring. I think the neighbors three doors down could hear her squealing from our kitchen. Then it was hugs all around, and even Benjamin came wandering in, still wearing his PJ bottoms and a T-shirt. "What's wrong?" he asked sleepily. "Why are you screaming down here?"

"Caitlin and Josh are engaged!" announced my mom.

He rolled his eyes. "Oh, is that all?"

"Hey, this is pretty big news," said Dad.

"News?" Ben just shook his head. "Not to me."

"Yeah, yeah," I told him. "You and Chloe Miller. You

both knew it was going to happen." I grinned at my little brother, who's actually not so little anymore. Ben towers above me and is a junior in high school now. "I can't wait to hear Chloe saying, 'I told you so.'"

"Congrats anyway," said Ben. "Josh is a good guy."

Then the phone rang.

"I'm sure that's for you," Mom said as she poured herself a cup of coffee.

And she was right. It was Beanie wanting the full lowdown. I took the phone to my room and filled her in on all the details.

"And what about the ring?" she said suddenly. "Did you like it?"

"I love it."

"I'm so happy for you guys."

"And you know that I want you as my maid of honor, Beanie."

"Really?"

"Of course! Didn't we promise each other back in middle school?"

"Yes, but I wouldn't hold you to it..."

"Beanie! You're my best friend."

"And you're mine too, Caitlin. I just know that you have a lot of good friends. Who else are you going to have in the wedding?"

"Good question. Naturally, I'll want Chloe."

"Oh, yeah. What about Allie and Laura?"

"Well, I love those two, but I was thinking maybe I should ask Jenny, and I wondered about Aunt Steph, since I was in her wedding. And then there's Anna, and I was even considering Liz." I sighed. "I guess I better think this thing over. It's not like I want thirteen bridesmaids."

"That would be some wedding."

"At least I know for sure who I want standing up next to me, Beanie."

"Thanks. That means a lot to me."

Later on this morning, Josh picked me up for church. And once I was in his car, I remember feeling just totally amazed that I was actually sitting next to the man I was going to marry. It's still so incredibly unbelievable.

"How are you doing?" he asked in a somewhat tentative voice, like maybe he was still wondering if last night was for real.

I smiled. "Great. How about you?"

"I feel like I'm having this fantastic dream." Then he peered at me. "You haven't changed your mind, have you?"

I laughed. "Not hardly!"

"How did your shoes fare?"

I laughed again. "Not so well. But, hey, it was worth it."

"Guess I should've told you to wear galoshes."

Then we were at church. And we were barely through the front door when everyone started congratulating us. Between Chloe and Beanie, the big news had spread through the congregation like wildfire. Josh had to head downstairs for the high school group. But I was still getting slaps on the back and showing off my ring and generally having a great time as I went with Beanie and Aunt Steph to the adult class in the fellowship room behind the sanctuary.

"Tell me everything," insisted Steph.

"Better make it fast," Beanie said as the leader started heading for the podium.

And so, I gave Aunt Steph the nutshell version of last night's picnic in the rain. Then we got hushed by Robert Martin (the leader) because the three of us were giggling like thirteen-year-olds.

"I know there's some excitement in the air." He smiled directly at me. "But some of us would still like to hear today's lesson." And really, I tried to concentrate on his teaching from Philippians, but I'm afraid I was mostly daydreaming. I'm just glad there wasn't a test afterward.

And then, of course, Pastor Tony insisted that Josh and I stand up in front of the whole congregation during the main service—although I'm sure that everyone probably knew about us by then. But it was fun hearing their applause and hoots of delight. And once again, it made me so glad that we'd waited until the timing was really right. You just can't beat perfect timing.

It was Josh's idea to get our two families together before I went back to school later today. "Sort of an engagement celebration," he explained to my parents and Ben after church. "I already called my folks, and they want to meet us at Renaldo's around one, if that works for you guys."

I'm not sure why I felt so anxious about this little

get-together. I mean, I already know Josh's parents, and I really do like them. But I suppose his mom still makes me nervous. It's not that she's not nice; she definitely is. And she's actually a lot nicer than she used to be. I think she likes me, or at least she acts as if she does.

But even so, she's a lot more formal than my mom. She's very into manners and appearances, and she's kind of a perfectionist who always dresses just so, with pearls and matching purses and shoes, and every hair in place. As a result, I feel somewhat inferior around her. I guess I'll have to get over that.

"Caitlin," she said as she took my hand in hers. "You're looking lovely as usual."

I smiled. "You are too, Mrs. Miller."

"Oh, you can't keep calling me Mrs. Miller now." She nodded to her husband. "From now on it's Joy and Stan."

"That's right," Josh's dad said as he gave me a hug. "You're part of the family now."

"She's always been part of the family," said Chloe.

Soon the eight of us were seated around a big table, and before long, Josh and I were retelling the story of the soggy picnic in the park. I actually think it gets better with each telling.

"Let's see that ring," Joy said as our tale came to an end.

I extended my hand across the table and waited as she examined it, slightly worried that it might not pass the test. I mean, just because I think it's perfect...but what do I know about fine jewelry?

"Beanie helped Josh pick it out," my mom explained in an almost apologetic tone. Maybe she wasn't too sure either.

"It's exquisite," Joy finally said, and I sighed in relief.

"Have you kids set a date yet?" asked my dad.

"Not exactly," said Josh. "I tried to talk her into eloping last night, but she told me to forget it." He winked at me.

"I was thinking maybe June," I said.

"Naturally, Caitlin wants to finish school and graduate," added Josh.

"The only problem is that we'd both wanted to get down to Mexico in early June," I told them. "And that kind of cuts into the honeymoon."

"Maybe you could have your honeymoon down there," suggested my dad. "Might save some travel time."

"In Mexico?" Joy frowned at my dad, as if he'd just recommended we stay in a cheap motel in downtown Tijuana.

"They have some nice resorts down there," my mom said with a slightly stiff smile. "On the beach."

"I suppose."

"I think a resort in Mexico is a great idea," said Josh quickly. "I'll have to go on-line and look into the possibilities."

"They've been having some real bargains lately," offered my dad. "And if that doesn't work, I've heard that cruises are getting cheaper every day."

"Not a cruise for the kids." Joy firmly shook her head.

"That's for old people like us."

"Sounds good to me," said Stan.

"Now," Joy said, turning her attention back to my mom. "We'll need to start planning for the big event right away."

"Right away?" My mom looked skeptical. "But it's only October."

"Well, a June wedding is right around the corner," said Joy. "And there's so much to be done in just a few months. There are invitations and dresses and flowers and photographers and, of course, the reception." She turned to her husband. "Stan, don't you think the country club would be absolutely perfect for a June reception? We'll have to book it right away."

Suddenly my parents looked fairly overwhelmed, and I started to feel slightly guilty. We've never really talked about anything like this before, and I had no idea how involved they wanted to be in my wedding plans. I wasn't even sure how involved I wanted them to be. The truth is, this was all still new to me.

"Don't worry," Joy said in a calm voice. "I helped my sister plan a wedding for my niece a few years ago. It's not terribly complicated if you start early enough. I think I still have a book that lists everything that must be done and when it's time to do it." She smiled at me now. "Don't you worry about a thing, Caitlin. Your mother and I will have everything under control before you even know it."

I think that's when I first started to worry.

Monday, October 24

Josh assured me that he'd get his mother to calm down about the wedding as he drove me back to college yesterday afternoon.

"I know she means well," I said. "But isn't the bride's family supposed to handle most of the wedding plans?"

He laughed. "You know my mom. She loves to get her finger into this kind of thing. I still remember Aunt Kathy wanting to pull her hair out because my mom insisted on having these specially engraved wedding favors for all the guests, and they ended up costing a small fortune. My aunt still won't let her forget about that."

"And you need to remember that my parents aren't as well-off as yours."

"It's ironic too," he said. "Because I'll bet your dad makes more than my dad. It's just that my family has inherited a lot of their money, and my mom's pretty good with investments. Plus, there's Chloe and all her recording contracts that get my mom to thinking we're millionaires."

"But that's Chloe's money, Josh."

"But she's a very generous girl."

I wanted to get back to the wedding subject. "Well, anyway, I hope things don't get out of control. I'm not even sure what my parents can afford. Things might need to stay simple."

"I'll do my best to hold my mom back while you're away," he told me as we finally pulled up to my dorm building. "But we will have to make some decisions,

Caitlin. As far as finals and graduation go, look at your calendar, then e-mail me when you think you've got the date narrowed down."

Then Josh walked me up the steps to my dorm, holding my hand more tightly as we reached the door. "I don't want to let you go," he said as we stood outside and hugged.

"I don't want to go."

"You sure you don't want to elope with me after all?" he teased.

I pretended to consider this, then firmly shook my head. "No way, Josh. I've waited a long time for this. I want a wedding with all the bells and whistles." Then I paused. "Well, maybe not all the bells and whistles, and certainly not those expensive engraved guest gifts. But I definitely want the white gown and all my friends and family gathered to celebrate with us."

He smiled and pulled me closer to him. "That's what I want too."

"But I don't know about a reception at the country club."

His face was close to mine now. "Me neither."

And then we kissed. Believe it or not, it was only our second kiss since I'd agreed to marry him. One was on the porch at my house the previous night. And then tonight. But it was a long and passionate kiss and by the time we finished, I felt light-headed, like I could barely breathe. Then we hugged tightly for a long time. And finally Josh sighed and just looked down at me. "I think it might be a good thing we're not living in the same town, Caitlin," he said in a husky voice.

I smiled at him. "Too tough to resist me?"

He laughed. "It's always been tough to resist you."

"Same back at you." I reached up and touched his cheek, studying his face so I could dream about him tonight.

Just then the door shot open, and several girls came bursting out. They were arguing about where they were going for pizza, and it seemed pretty clear that our romantic moment was lost.

"I'll e-mail you when I get home," said Josh.

I nodded, feeling sad to see him leave. "I'll miss you."

"I love you," he said in a quiet voice.

"I love you too."

And then he was gone. I suppose he might be right about the distance thing. In some ways it is a relief knowing that we won't always be peeling ourselves off of each other. And despite the fact that I know he IS the one and I fully intend to marry this guy, I still do NOT plan to sleep with him—or to have any form of sex with him—until our wedding night.

Call me old-fashioned or conservative or just a woman who's trying to obey God, but I am committed to this. Even so, I won't deny that those old hot-and-tingly feelings were rushing all through me. I'd have to be dead not to notice.

DEAR GOD, PLEASE HELP JOSH AND ME TO LIVE
OUT OUR ENGAGEMENT IN A WAY THAT HONORS
YOU. AND HELP US TO FIGURE OUT THE BEST
WEDDING DATE AND THE KIND OF PLANS THAT
EVERYONE WILL ENJOY AND APPRECIATE. MOST OF
ALL, HELP ME TO KEEP MY HEART TUNED IN TO
YOU ABOVE ALL ELSE. AMEN.

THREE

Tuesday, October 25

At the beginning of this school year, Jenny Lambert called to tell me that she had transferred to the university and was looking for a roommate. The timing couldn't have been better, since my old roommate Liz Banks had already moved in with her new boyfriend, and I was temporarily roommate-less.

And even though I was seriously bummed to lose Liz (despite all the challenges in the past), it was great getting to hang with Jenny again. I'd almost forgotten how much fun we'd had during our senior year in high school. And here we would be doing it all over again in our senior year of college. Not only that, but Jenny can be such fun. Whereas Liz can be dark and moody at times (plus she's not a Christian); Jenny is usually bubbly and light, and she's a Christian.

When I got home on Sunday night, Jenny had been out late, so I wasn't actually able to share my big news until

after classes on Monday. I decided to invite her to fish
and chips, where I thought we could celebrate my
engagement. But when I asked her, she told me that she
wasn't really hungry. Now this kind of bothered me, since
she seems to be "not hungry" a lot lately, and I guess I'm
still a little worried that she may still be playing with the
whole anorexia thing.

Now I haven't asked her about this specifically yet. I
mean, we've only been rooming together for a few weeks,
and it's possible that I'm just feeling overly sensitive since
I'm still wearing the "freshman fifteen." (It's supposed to
only be five, but that's how many pounds I've put on since
I started college!)

Okay, I'll admit that I was a little underweight at
the beginning of my freshman year, but these extra
pounds have been bugging me lately. Maybe even more so
now that I'm engaged. I kept thinking I'd start working
out or jogging, but I get so loaded with classes and stuff
that I forget. And when I saw Jenny this fall, just as
skinny as ever, well, I suppose I felt a little envious. And
that might've been what made me suspicious about the
whole anorexia thing again. Seriously, I hope she's not.

"But I wanted to go out to celebrate," I told her.

"Celebrate?" She looked curious.

"Yes. Don't you think you could get hungry for that?"

She seemed to consider this. "I suppose I could eat a
salad."

Trying to put anorexia fears behind me, I agreed to

this, and we headed over to the fish-and-chip place.
Then feeling too guilty to order fish and chips while I was
with skinny Jenny who only wanted salad, I followed her
lead and ordered light. But at least I had shrimp on my
salad. After we got seated, I told her my news, and
naturally she was very happy for me.

"Josh is a good guy, Cate." She stuck a straw into her
diet soda.

Hearing her call me Cate again, I had to smile.
Somehow Jenny's always gotten away with that nick-
name. "I agree," I said.

"Even though he and I had some difficult times, you
know, way back when..." She forced a little laugh. "I still
think he's a great guy."

Just as the waitress set down our salads, I suddenly
remembered that Jenny and Josh had gone out during
high school. I mean, it was only briefly, and so long ago...so
much water under the bridge. It was almost as if I'd forgotten. Or like it had never happened.

But it had.

"I almost forgot," I admitted to her.

She smiled. "Yeah, me too."

"Does it bother you?"

Jenny shook her head. "No. Not at all."

"Good." I picked up my fork, relieved, but suddenly
wishing I'd ordered fish and chips since I really was hungry. I could just imagine how good they'd be all soaked in
vinegar.

"You two are so right for each other," she continued. "I always knew you'd get married someday."

"Really?"

"Sure. Everyone did." She reached over and squeezed my hand. "I'm so happy for you, Cate."

"Thanks."

And okay, I think she meant it. But there's this part of me that's not sure. I mean, Jenny is so good at keeping a cheerful front. How do I know if she's really okay with this? And I watched her "eating" last night. She picked and picked at her salad, but by the time we left, she'd only consumed a few pieces of the lettuce.

I think I'll have to ask her about the anorexia thing. And if she really is struggling with this again, part of me is going to feel angry, and I know that's totally unfair. But when I agreed to be roommates, that's not what I signed on for. I don't want to have to confront her or watch her or worry about her starving to death.

To be honest, I just want her to be the normal, happy Jenny that everyone loves. I want her to be my buddy and maybe even help me make some plans for the wedding, because everyone knows that Jenny has really good taste. I want her to be glad that I'm engaged to the guy I love and to be supportive. Most of all, and I know this is totally selfish, I don't want her to rain on my parade. But really, how egotistic is that?

DEAR GOD, PLEASE HELP ME TO BE A BETTER
FRIEND TO JENNY. HELP ME TO KNOW WHAT TO
SAY IF SHE'S HAVING PROBLEMS WITH ANOREXIA.
HELP ME TO SHOW HER HOW MUCH I LOVE HER AND
CARE ABOUT HER. HELP ME REMEMBER THAT MY
ENGAGEMENT TO JOSH IS NOT THE CENTER OF
THE UNIVERSE. AMEN.

Wednesday, October 26

Even though Liz and I aren't rooming together anymore, I
still believe that our friendship is good for the long haul. I
mean, after all we've been through these past three
years, I think we should be able to survive almost anything. Of course, I did my best trying to talk her out of
what I thought was a totally stupid move on her part.
But then Liz has always been a girl to make up her own
mind, and, as sad as it is, she seems to enjoy learning
things the hard way.

And so I must admit, I was pretty bummed when I
found out about her and Leon. I really thought she'd
gotten more open to God last year. I guess I actually felt
it was just a matter of time before she would make
some kind of commitment. Then Leon comes along (he's
doing a master's program here), and he sweeps her off
her feet. And the next thing you know, she's moved in
with him. Now I'm not saying Leon isn't a nice guy. He
actually seems rather thoughtful. But considering Liz's
record with guys, it's hard to tell this early in the game.

"Don't worry, Caitlin," she teased me, shortly after I'd heard their news. "I won't let Leon come between us."

"But I'll still miss you."

"At least you have Jenny now," said Liz. I could tell right from the start that Liz didn't like Jenny.

"She's exactly what I thought you were when I first met you," Liz told me privately, after I'd introduced her to my new roommate. It was one of those Liz double-whammy kind of insults. She's an expert at it.

"But you were wrong about me," I reminded her.

"But I'm right about Jenny."

"Come on, Liz. I thought you'd gotten more open-minded than this."

"Maybe I'm just jealous," she said.

I laughed. "Yeah. If anyone should be jealous, it should be me. You left me for Leon long before I even knew Jenny was transferring here."

"Oh, you probably would've dumped me for her anyway." But I could tell by the spark in her eye that she was just doing her typical chain-jerking now.

"Yeah, right."

But at least we agreed to have a weekly coffee date—every Tuesday at seven—just to keep up.

And so I got to tell her my big news last night. I couldn't wait to hear her reaction. Especially since she's always telling me that what I need is a good boyfriend. Of course, I know by this she means sex. But that's just her.

"No way!" Liz shrieked so loudly that everyone in Starbucks jumped.

"Shh." I waved my ring finger in front of her face to quiet her down.

"Oh-mi-gosh!" She stared at the ring, then looked up at me with disbelief. "This is the real deal."

"The real deal." I grinned.

"And you know without a doubt that Josh is really 'the one.'"

"I think I've always known."

She rolled her eyes. "What a hopeless romantic."

I shrugged. "Hey, someone has to be."

"Well, don't even ask me how it's going with Leon."

"How's it going?"

"I said don't ask."

"But I thought you meant—"

"I meant, don't ask."

I nodded. "Okay then." And so, trying to avoid the Leon subject, I began to tell her about the engagement picnic and how it rained and how I ruined my new shoes, but the whole time I could tell that something was troubling her. Finally, I couldn't stand it any longer.

"Liz," I began carefully. "You don't have to talk about it, but I know you too well. I know that something's really wrong."

She sighed and looked away. "Oh, I don't know..."

"Is it Leon?" I felt myself getting mad now. "Is he cheating on you, Liz?"

She frowned, but knowing Liz's history with picking out guys who are total jerks, I knew this was a very real possibility. But she just mutely shook her head.

"He's <u>not</u> cheating?"

"No."

"Oh." Now I was at a loss. "But you seem so sad."

She sighed again. "Look, Leon is really great, Caitlin. He's good to me. He's thoughtful. He's probably the best boyfriend I've ever had."

Now it's hard to respond to something like that. On one hand, I'm relieved that Leon's not another stupid jerk. But on the other hand, I feel as though she's settling for less than God's best for her. But then again it's not like she's even invited God into her life, so she obviously has no idea what He has to offer.

Really, it can be so frustrating trying to encourage someone in this position. It's like you're telling them about this really great restaurant while you know they have no money and will refuse to accept charity. Just the same, I love Liz too much to say nothing. I mean, I pray for her all the time. And I honestly believe God has a fantastic plan for her life. If she'd only just get it.

"So, if Leon's so great...what's the problem, Liz?"

"I think it's me."

"Oh." I watched her as she swirled the last of her coffee around in the bottom of the cup. "Are you cheating on him?" I finally asked what seemed like the obvious next question.

I felt somewhat relieved that this made her laugh. "No, I'm not cheating. Thanks for the vote of confidence."

"Well, it's not as if you've never done anything like that before."

"Yeah, you're right. But believe it or not, I've grown up a little since then."

I nodded. "I know. So really, what's wrong?"

"I don't know exactly. It's just that there's something missing. Like maybe Leon's not really the one. Not the way Josh seems to be the one for you anyway." Now she stared at me, giving me that same narrow-eyed skeptical look that I've grown so familiar with over the past three years. "I'll bet you guys still haven't even slept together."

I laughed. "That's a bet you could make some money on. Of course, you might be hard-pressed to get anyone to bet against you."

"And I suppose you don't plan on sleeping together until the big white night?"

"That's right."

She shook her head as she let out a cuss word, then quickly apologized. Not that I was shocked. I mean, since I've known her, Liz has always had a mouth on her.

"It's just that I believe God has led me to live like this, Liz," I explained for like the hundredth time. "And I'm glad. Really, waiting works for me."

"Yeah, yeah. I know the spiel."

"Okay, Liz, if you don't think Leon is the one, and it's not working...then why are you still with him?"

"Convenience, I guess."

I nodded as I considered her response. "I suppose it might seem convenient."

"What do you mean by that?"

"Oh, you know. It <u>seems</u> like the easy thing to do, like it doesn't matter one way or the other, like it all works out in the end. But you know as well as anyone that you always have to pay in the end. I mean, either you get hurt, or the guy gets hurt, or you both get hurt. It's always the same, Liz."

"I guess."

"And what if?" I suddenly thought of something.

"What if what?"

"Well, what if there really is a right guy for you? I mean, what if some amazing guy is made just for you, but you are so busy being in a <u>convenient</u> relationship that you totally miss it? What if?"

She frowned. "Yeah, you bet. Some Mr. Right is out there looking for me even as we speak."

"You don't know, Liz; he could be. He might be here right now." Then I did this scope-it-out glance, like I was trying to see if any cool-looking guy might be sitting right there in Starbucks, and Liz just laughed.

"And you think I'll miss Mr. Right because I'm stuck with Leon."

"Maybe."

"Okay, let's just suppose your theory holds water, which I seriously doubt. How am I supposed to recognize this perfect dude when I see him anyway? Will he have a sign on his forehead or maybe a T-shirt that says Mr. Right across his massive chest?"

"I think you'll only get the answer to that question once you've hooked up with God, Liz."

She nodded with this knowing look. "Yeah, I figured we'd end up here before long."

I shrugged. "Hey, you know who I am."

But instead of getting irritated, she just smiled. "Yeah, and it's kind of nice that you never let me down either."

So now I realize that I have a couple of friends whose lives aren't going so well. And it reminds me that I need to keep thinking about other people and not get so focused on my own life. I mean, it's cool that Josh and I are getting married. But right now I'm still in college. I still have friends who need me to be here for them. And I need to lean on God for my strength more than ever. I guess it was sort of a wake-up call. In other words, and as usual, it's not all about me.

DEAR GOD, THANKS FOR REMINDING ME THAT MY LIFE ISN'T JUST ABOUT BEING ENGAGED TO A WONDERFUL GUY. HELP ME TO KEEP MY EYES ON YOU AND TO BE THERE FOR MY FRIENDS. SHOW ME HOW I CAN HELP BOTH LIZ AND JENNY. AMEN.

FOUR

Saturday, October 29

Josh drove over to the university to pick me up from school yesterday. I can't believe how glad I was to see him. It seemed like it had been more than a mere five days since we'd been together. After I hugged him for about five minutes (or maybe just two), I told him the official date for our wedding.

"How does the first of June sound?"

"Sounds perfect."

"My graduation is May 27," I told him. "And I know that's packing it in pretty close, less than a week to get home and do all the last-minute wedding things, but wouldn't it be great to be down at the mission by mid-June?"

"Does that mean we get a two-week honeymoon?"

I laughed. "Do you think we can afford two weeks?"

"Maybe if we find some fleabag motel down in Mexico or sleep on the beach."

"Wow, that sounds so romantic."

He grinned. "Hey, if it was with you, it would be very romantic."

Well, I'm sure that made me blush, so I quickly changed the subject. "You can't pick me up and take me home every weekend," I said as we entered the freeway.

"Why not?"

"Believe me, I'm not complaining. Leaving in the afternoon like this is great for me, since I only have morning classes on Fridays. But you have a job, and it eats up a lot of your time to drive back and forth like this, Josh. Really, I don't expect it."

"I know. And you're right. I probably won't be able to do it every weekend. But I just had to see you again. For one thing, I kept worrying that none of this was real."

"But we e-mailed."

"I know. But I needed to see you with my own eyes, Caitlin."

I smiled. "Like I said, I'm not complaining."

And believe me, I am totally glad to be home again. Everyone here is so excited about the engagement and the upcoming wedding. It's a total departure from what's going on back at school. To be honest, I sort of feel like a princess when I come home. My mom sat me down with some ideas for the wedding. Okay, some were a little corny, like craft projects she might be better off doing with her second graders at school.

Then Josh's mom invited my mom and me for lunch

today, and afterward we went to a new bridal shop to
look at wedding gowns. And even though I don't agree
with Joy's ideas that "money shouldn't matter" when it
comes to getting the perfect dress, I must admit that
she has pretty good taste.

"You are a classic, Caitlin," she told me as she held
up this beautiful white satin gown. "You'll look best in
something smooth and sophisticated like this."

"I'm not sure about strapless." I held up the gown in
front of the mirror. Although as I admired how the gown
flowed gracefully to the floor, I was sure I could be
talked into this style.

"I'm with you, Caitlin," my mom said quickly. "I think
something with a little more shoulder would be nice." She
had already removed another dress from the rack. And
okay, I have to admit it looked a little too fluffy and
prissy to me. But I smiled as I held it up in the mirror.

"Oh, that'd be so sweet on you," said my mom.

"No, no," said Joy. "It's much too ingénue for her."

"Ingénue?" my mom queried.

"Too young. Too sweet. Too little girlish."

My mom just looked at her.

"But don't worry," said Joy. "This is only one store and
a small one at that." I kind of smiled at the sales girl
who'd been trying to help us.

"And I'm sure Caitlin has lots of time," said my mom.

"If we go into the city, we'll have lots more gowns to
choose from," said Joy. "I only thought that Caitlin should
start looking at styles so she'll have some idea of what

she's looking for." Joy pulled out another dress and held it
up, but it looked more like an evening gown to me.

"Do you want to try anything on, honey?" My mom's
voice strongly hinted that she was ready to leave.

"Not really." I glanced at my watch. "Lunch was nice
and this was fun, but I told Aunt Steph that I'd stop by
and visit her this afternoon."

My mom smiled as she hung the princess dress back up.

"Oh, I almost forgot," said Joy. "I have some wedding
things for you, Caitlin. They're in my car."

The "wedding things" turned out to be a slick shopping bag full of new brides' magazines and several thick,
glossy "wedding planning" books that appear to cover
everything from French pedicures to appropriate ice
sculptures. Not only that, but Joy went to the trouble to
stick little Post-it notes on various pages that she felt
were good ideas. Of course, I didn't actually look
through these things until I was in the privacy of my own
room. No need rubbing my mom's nose in it.

So, I can see this isn't going to be easy. And I don't
really want to complain to Josh about his mother's input. I
realize she's just trying to help. And to be fair, she does
have some good ideas, and her taste (well, other than
those big-ticket items) is probably more like mine than my
mother's. Naturally, I can't admit this to Mom.

That's what made me decide to ask Aunt Steph's
opinion while I'm at her house. After I tell her my little
story of the wedding gown skirmish, and after she recov-
ers from laughing, she reminds me that it's my wedding.

"Well, yours and Josh's." She cradles little Clayton on her lap. He's about three years old now and appears to be nearly asleep. "He missed his nap today," she whispers as she gracefully moves him to the couch. Then she stands up and sighs. "Of course, a wedding is about families too."

"I know. And really, I want everyone to be happy and have a good time. But I think it's going to be tricky."

She sits back down across from me. "I guess you and Josh will have to settle on your priorities."

"Like what? You've helped with weddings at the church, Steph. What do you tell people to do?"

"Well, the weddings at our church are usually fairly simple affairs," she says. "Not everyone wants to get married in an old retail building."

I nod. "That's another thing. Josh's parents really want us to get married in their church."

"Is that Saint Matthew's?"

"Yes."

"It is a gorgeous old church, Caitlin. I just love the old stone and stained glass and all that wood in the sanctuary."

"I know, I know. But I want to be married at Faith Fellowship, and I want Pastor Tony to officiate."

"I suppose I'm a little biased, but I do think you should have Tony too." She smiles as she glances at the wedding picture of Tony and her on the mantel. "After all, he is family."

"Right. And he's also Josh's boss."

"That's true. But Saint Matthew's _is_ a beautiful church, Caitlin." She pauses to consider something. "Maybe you guys could compromise a little. Maybe Saint Matthew's would allow Tony to do the ceremony there."

"Do you think?"

She shrugs. "He's done weddings in other churches. I could ask him about it."

"But nothing's decided yet. I still need to talk to Josh. In fact, maybe I should let him handle it since he lives here and sees Tony every day."

"Good thinking." She smiles. "I'm sure you're busy with school. Maybe you should just delegate everything you can for this wedding."

"But I want to be involved."

"Of course. But you've got lots of people who love you, Caitlin. You might as well let us help."

"But what if Josh's mom takes over?"

Aunt Steph laughs. "Between your mom and me, and hey, we can even pull your grandmother into the fray, I think Mrs. Miller will have her work cut out for her."

We talk some more and finally Aunt Steph encourages me to start making lists. "And talk to your parents about the finances. You'll have no idea what you can or cannot do until you know what kind of budget is involved."

"Good point."

And so this evening I sit down with my parents and asked them about money. "I hate to even bring this up," I begin somewhat apologetically. "But Aunt Steph says we need to discuss it."

"She's right," says my dad. Then he gets this sad expression. "And I wish I could say that I've got it all covered, honey. But I've been doing a little research on the cost of weddings..." He shakes his head.

"It's unbelievable what a wedding costs these days," says my mom. "I had no idea."

"What does a wedding cost?" I ask, realizing that perhaps I should've checked this out already.

"According to several web sites, the average wedding is about twenty-five grand." My dad seems to be studying my face now.

"Twenty-five grand?" I'm sure my eyes are popping out of my head just now. "Twenty-five thousand dollars?" I repeat the freaking figure one more time just to make sure I'm getting this right. "For one single day? Not even a whole day, just a few hours? Man, that sounds more like the down payment on a house or a couple of years' worth of tuition. Are you sure, Dad?"

"And that's just the average cost. I guess a lot of weddings are even more."

"Maybe Josh is onto something," I say suddenly. "Maybe we should elope."

"No, honey." My mom frowns. "We'll figure this out somehow."

"But no way are we spending that much money," I say. "I think that's crazy."

"If you look at how it all breaks down," says Dad, "you'll see that it all manages to add up."

"But I don't need to have everything. We can keep

things simple. I mean, like the dress. I've heard they go for thousands, but I'd never want a dress like that."

My mom sighs. "That's a relief."

"And we can cut corners," I continue. "Elise Curtis got her wedding cake from a grocery store."

"Oh, we don't need to be that cheap," says my dad. "Besides, I plan to invite associates from the office, Caitlin. Everyone there still remembers you."

"Dad, twenty-five grand is outrageous."

My mom nods. "We don't have that kind of money just sitting around."

"We've been talking about refinancing our house."

"Not for a wedding, Dad!"

"No, not just for a wedding," Mom explains. "It would be for paying off some bills and consolidating our finances, and there'd probably be enough left over for an inexpensive wedding." She looks slightly deflated. "Oh, we'd love to give you the best wedding ever, honey. You know we would."

"That's true," agrees Dad. "If anyone deserves a big, fancy wedding, it's you, sweetheart."

"I don't want a big fancy wedding. I just want it to be nice and something we'll always remember."

"We thought you'd understand," says Dad. "You've always been a sensible girl."

"I hope that Josh's mother understands," says Mom.

"If she doesn't, maybe she'd like to chip in about ten grand or so," Dad suggests with a twinkle in his eye.

My mom socks him in the arm. "You're terrible, Mike!"

"Well, Joy needs to understand what we can and cannot do."

"Don't worry about it," I tell them. "I'll warn Josh that this wedding has to stay within a very strict budget. You tell me what can be spent, and we'll stick to it."

"Okay," says my dad. "We'll work some numbers out on paper and let you know."

"And really," I assure them. "I know it's all going to be just fine. God knows what we need for a wedding, and I believe He'll provide for it. And if we end up repeating our vows in the backyard with hot dogs for a reception, it's fine with me."

"Good grief, I hope not," says Mom. "I'd have to hire a landscaper and—"

"Stop, stop!" I hold up my hands. "I was just kidding."

Sunday, October 30

I explain the financial situation to Josh as he drives me back to school.

"You're kidding!" he says after I tell him the cost of the average wedding. "Twenty-five thousand bucks? That's insane."

"I know. That's what I thought too. But after my parents told me, I did a little research of my own, and it's true. You look at an itemized list, and it all adds up pretty fast. Of course, I think there are lots of ways to save money and cut corners."

"I hope so."

"And if you ask me, weddings have gotten pretty commercialized, and everyone's trying to get rich off of the poor unsuspecting couple." I shake my head. "It's really awful if you think about it."

"What?"

"Well, about half of the marriages will end in divorce. Some only a couple of years after the wedding. Can you imagine shelling out that kind of money for a wedding that ends up in divorce court? What a waste."

Josh reaches over and puts his hand on my arm. "It'll never happen to us, Caitlin."

I nod. "But just the same, it makes you feel kind of sick to think of all the couples who invest that kind of money in a wedding and then don't even make it in a marriage."

"That's one of the reasons that Tony is starting to teach marriage classes. He invited us to participate in the first one."

"When does it start?"

"In January."

"Does he know what days it will be?"

"No, but I have a feeling he could work it into something that fits your schedule."

"Like maybe during the weekend?"

"Yeah, and that'll give me an even better excuse for coming to pick you up all the time." He frowns now. "And that reminds me, I won't be able to make it next weekend. Friday is a no-school day, and the youth group is doing a two-day workathon for FAD." (Of course, I know what he means since this is the acronym I made up several years ago. FAD stands for Food At the Dump, and it's our church's organization for sending money to the mission in Mexico to be used specifically for the kids who live at the dump.)

"Hey, that's cool, Josh."

"You don't mind?"

"Of course not. I think it's awesome that you're raising money for the kids. Besides, a weekend on campus will give me time to catch up on my schoolwork."

"You mean you're behind?"

"Not exactly. But I don't mind getting a little ahead either."

"Well then, I wanted to ask if you could make it for the ski retreat. It's the first weekend after New Year's. I thought maybe you could play the role of the girls' counselor."

I start to giggle as I recall a certain ski retreat that happened about five years ago.

"What's so funny about that?" he asks.

"Do you remember that ski retreat when we first hooked up in high school?"

"Do I remember?" He laughs. "I still have good dreams about it."

"Yeah, but as I recall you really set me back on my search for God. I was trying to figure out my life, and you totally derailed me with your passionate make-out sessions."

He sighs. "Hey, I could get into that again."

And the next thing I know, he pulls off the road, and we are making out like a couple of sixteen-year-olds. Finally, we're both breathing so hard that the windows are fogged up, and I realize that this has to stop.

"Josh," I say in a quiet but firm voice.

"I know." He pulls himself away and starts the engine again. "But oh, was it worth it."

"If we keep that up, we'll have to elope," I tell him in what I hope he knows is a nonserious voice.

"Works for me."

"I guess it could save money."

"Would you even consider it?" He looks slightly alarmed now.

"No, silly. We have too many family and friends who are looking forward to this. And I am too, Josh. Really, I've always dreamed of this day."

"Yeah. Me too. Okay, let's agree—no eloping."

"Okay, but back to the wedding budget, Josh. I don't want to be a wet blanket, but we need to get this fact through to your mom. Our wedding has to stay within the budget my parents are comfortable with. Unfortunately, I think this means no reception at the country club."

"Unfortunately?" He laughs. "That sounds like great news to me."

"Well, your parents may be disappointed."

"Too bad. This is our wedding, Caitlin. We get to have some say on the decisions."

Finally, we're back in front of my dorm, and it's time to say good-bye again. And once again it's hard to let go.

It's like the closer we get, the more we spend time together, the harder it becomes to be apart.

"Someday we won't be saying good-bye like this all the time," I tell him as I finally pull away from his warm hug.

"It won't be too soon for me, Caitlin."

One more kiss and we go our separate ways.

DEAR GOD, I KNOW YOU'VE MADE US TO HAVE SEXUAL FEELINGS. AND I KNOW THAT SOMEDAY WE'LL GET TO EXPERIENCE THE WHOLE ENCHILADA. BUT UNTIL THEN, I PLEDGE MYSELF TO REMAIN PURE FOR YOU—AND FOR JOSH TOO. HELP US TO STICK TO OUR CONVICTIONS. AMEN.

FIVE

Thursday, November 3

Jenny's been sick the last two days, and I can't help but think it has to do with her eating habits. I decided to confront her on this tonight.

"I'm worried about you," I tell her after I bring her a hot bowl of tomato soup that I made for her myself down in the kitchen. Okay, it was from a can, but it took me some time. But now she refuses to touch it.

"It's just the flu," she says.

I sit on her bed and put my hand on her shoulder. "Jenny, I think it's more than the flu."

"What do you mean?"

"I mean, I think you're not eating."

I can tell by the way she looks away, avoiding my eyes, that I must be right. "It's true, isn't it, Jenny?"

She just shrugs.

"Come on, Jenny, I know you. I went through this whole

thing with you in high school. Be honest with me. Okay?"

Then she looks at me, but there are tears in her eyes. "I thought I could handle it. I thought that rooming with you would help me."

"You mean you've been doing this for a while?"

"No, not really. It started in the summer."

"But why?"

"Why?" She swipes at the tears on her face. "If I knew why, I probably wouldn't be doing it, would I?"

"Just tell me what's going on. How did it begin?"

"It began the same way it always begins," she says in a flat voice. "With me."

"I know. But what triggered it?"

She tries to laugh, but it's not convincing. "My body triggered it. It started in August when I went with my parents to stay in their time-share in San Diego. I'd had a pretty stressful summer...you know, working and deciding whether I wanted to transfer here. So I was ready for a little downtime. About the first day there, I was at the pool with my mom, just lying around and trying to get a little tan going since I'd barely been outside all summer and was as white as a ghost. Then my mom makes this comment about how I'd put on a few pounds."

Suddenly I want to scream. How could her mother possibly say something like that after all Jenny's gone through? But I manage to keep my mouth shut and just wait for her to continue.

"Well, I looked down at my big white thighs and realized that she was right, and I decided—"

"Jenny," I interrupt her. "You have <u>never</u> had big thighs."

"No, really, you should've seen them, Cate. I was like this big, white beached whale."

I stand up now, really angry. Indignantly angry. "Jenny! You are so wrong. Your body image is totally twisted." And then I start taking off my outer clothes. Okay, I guess I am flipping out a little. But it's like I can't help it. Her words just got to me. Finally, I am down to my underwear.

"Okay, Jenny," I say as I stand there looking ridiculous. "Look at me. All right, can you see me clearly? I have put on like <u>fifteen pounds</u> since high school. Fifteen pounds. Okay? And even though I'd really like to take them off, and by the way, I can't believe I'm standing here exposing my flabby body to someone as skinny as you are, but it's to make a point. And that's to let you know that if I never take off this weight, if I go to my wedding still weighing what I weigh now, well, I'm going to be just fine."

"You look great."

"How can you say that?" I demand as I go and stand in front of the full-length mirror on our door. "I mean, look at me, Jenny. This is the most I've ever weighed, and you probably don't even weight a hundred pounds right now."

"It's different."

I turn around, and despite the fact that she doesn't feel well, I pull her out of bed and make her stand in front of the mirror. "Yeah, you bet it's different."

She has on a T-shirt and boxers that hang loosely

over skinny little legs. I reach over and pull up her T-shirt to reveal a caved-in stomach and ribs that are already showing. "Can't you see the difference here?" Then I actually turn sideways to reveal my less-than-flat tummy. I even make it stick out a little, just for effect. Okay, it's humiliating. But desperate times call for desperate measures. I look at her face and see that there seems to be a trace of recognition.

"Okay, Jenny, tell me the truth. Do you think I'm fat?"

"No, you're not fat, Caitlin."

"Plump?"

She shakes her head. "You look good. Really, you do. Oh, I can see you've put on a little weight. But it actually looks kind of good on you."

"Okay, whatever. But tell me this: Which one of us is fatter?"

She doesn't answer.

"Jenny, I want to know. I'm not humiliating myself like this just for the fun of it. Which one of us is heavier? Which one of us could actually use a little workout plan?" And really, as I stand there looking at my midsection, I want to cry too. How have I gotten so out of shape? But that's beside the point. "Come on, Jenny. Can't you see the difference here?"

Finally she nods, and I feel like I've won a huge victory. "Really?" I ask. "Are you telling the truth, or just trying to get me to lay off? Can you see it?"

"I can see it."

"Okay." Now I let go of her shirt and stand facing the mirror, staring directly into her eyes. "This is the deal, Jenny. I will not room with you if you're going to do this to yourself. I'm sorry, but I just can't. I love you, and I'd like to help you. But I cannot stand to watch you starving yourself. Do you understand?"

She nods again.

"So if this is what you're going to do to yourself, well, you might as well pack it all up tonight and get a new roommate tomorrow."

Now she starts crying even harder, and I feel like maybe I've stepped over the line. But it's the truth. I don't think I can handle this. I don't even think that God wants me to.

"Do you understand what I'm saying, Jenny?"

She nods, then turns around and gets back into her bed.

I sit back down beside her. "Do you want to keep being roommates?"

"Not if you don't want me."

"I didn't say that, Jenny. I _said_ I can't handle sharing a room with an anorexic. If you can stop this thing now, I want you to stay. Can you stop it?"

"I don't know…"

"I don't know isn't an answer."

"You know I don't want to be like this."

"Then you're willing to stop it?"

Jenny sits up and slowly nods. "I _do_ want to stop it."

"And are you willing to get help? I'm sure there's some-one in the counseling center who knows about this."

"Yeah. I picked up a flyer last week; I even put it in my purse."

"So, are you willing to go and talk to them?"

"I guess."

"That's not good enough, Jenny. Will you make an appointment?"

"Yes."

"And I'll help you if I can."

"Really?" She sounds skeptical.

"Yeah, but you have to do your part. I can't help you if you can't help yourself." Now I stop to think about this seriously. What exactly am I taking on here? I mean, this is already looking to be a jam-packed year with my double major and wedding plans. Can I really handle this thing with Jenny too?

"Look," I finally say. "I have an idea. But it will only work if we both agree to it and really commit."

"What's your idea?"

"Well, I'd really like to lose some of this weight before the wedding. I mean, I certainly don't plan to obsess over it, but it's something I want to do. How about if we get a scale in here? And we both do a weigh-in every night. Would you be willing?"

"Okay."

"The thing is, you have to be gaining weight. And over a fair amount of time, I need to be losing. We'll eat breakfast and dinner together, you can encourage me to eat less, and I can encourage you to eat more. Do you think that would work?"

"You want me to teach you to be anorexic?" I can tell by the gleam in her eyes that she's kidding.

"Don't even go there," I warn her.

"Sorry."

"So, are you in agreement with this?"

"Yeah, I think I am."

"Jenny, I need more than 'I think I am' from you. Either you are or you aren't."

"I am."

So we shake hands, and I remind her that if she flakes out on me, she'll have to move out immediately. Then I watch from where I'm doing my homework as she slowly spoons down nearly half a bowl of soup. I consider complimenting her on this accomplishment but decide that some of this will have to come from her.

Later on after I turn out the light and get into bed, Jenny asks if I'm asleep.

"Not quite."

"Well, I just wanted to say thanks."

"It's okay," I tell her.

"No, I really appreciate it. You're a true friend."

"Yeah. And so are you."

"And I promise not to tell anyone how bad you looked in your underwear tonight."

Then I throw my pillow at her, and we both end up laughing.

But before I drift to sleep, I pray for Jenny.

DEAR GOD, PLEASE STRENGTHEN JENNY AND
SHOW HER HOW TO CONQUER HER ANOREXIA
ONCE AND FOR ALL. AND PLEASE STRENGTHEN ME
SO I CAN ACTUALLY HELP HER WITHOUT GETTING
PULLED UNDER MYSELF. AMEN.

SIX

Saturday, November 5

Okay, just when I think I have a week-
end to kick back and relax (since Josh isn't coming), I get
a phone call first thing this morning—it's his mother.

"Hi, Caitlin," she says in a chirpy voice. "I hope I didn't
wake you."

I glance at the clock to see that it's nearly nine. "No,
I was just getting up." Okay, it's a lie. But how do you
admit to your perfect mother-in-law to be that you've a
lazy bum?

"Well, I was thinking that since Josh is still doing that
workathon thing with the kids, perhaps this is a good day
for you and me to do something. Did you have plans,
dear?"

"No, not really."

"Oh, good. I'll leave right away and get there before
noon. We can run into the city, look at some bridal gowns,
and then have lunch."

"I—uh—is my mother coming?" I ask uncertainly. I mean, I know it would hurt my mom's feelings if I actually found the perfect dress with Josh's mom. But how do I tell her this?

"No, dear, I thought it would be nice to spend this time getting acquainted with you. Is that all right?"

"Sure, that sounds nice." Then I hang up and feel like a hypocrite.

"Who was that?" Jenny asks me sleepily.

"Josh's mom."

Jenny laughs.

"Why is that so funny?"

"Oh, just that she is so much like my mom. I guess I feel a little sorry for you."

"Thanks a lot."

"But at least your parents aren't like that."

"That's true, but you should see how exciting it gets when Josh's mom and my mom are talking about wedding decisions. I mean, my mom thinks that things like home-made crepe-paper flowers would look cute on the chairs that line the aisle, and naturally Joy wouldn't settle for anything less than hothouse roses and silk ribbons that were hand dyed in France. Honestly, she actually marked a page in a brides' magazine showing this. No way did I show that to my mom."

Jenny laughs even louder now. "So what does Josh's mom want with you today?"

"To look at bridal gowns."

"Oh, fun. Wish I could come."

I consider this. Having Jenny along could prove a good buffer, and besides, she has excellent taste. "Why don't you?" I say suddenly.

"Seriously?"

"Yes. I'd love to have you along."

"But would Mrs. Miller mind?"

"Maybe. But—" I stand dramatically now—"this isn't about her," I say in an affected voice. "It's about me. It's all about me."

Jenny throws a dirty sock in my face, and we both laugh.

"Oh, yeah," I add. "If you're going to come, you have to eat a big breakfast. I don't want you fainting on me."

"It's a deal," she says. And then down in the dining room, she actually does a decent job of putting away a bowl of Cheerios with banana slices on top. And feeling encouraged by this, I decide to bring up what I've been thinking about for the past couple of weeks. I glance around to see that the room is nearly empty. Probably due to the fact that the rest of the girls in the dorm didn't get a wake-up call from their fiancé's mother this morning.

"I've been meaning to ask you something," I say as I pour myself another cup of coffee and sit back down.

"What?"

"Would you be a bridesmaid in my wedding?"

Jenny looks surprised. "Of course. I'd love to, Cate. Are you serious?"

"Yes, I want you there with me."

"Who else are you having?"

"So far it's just Beanie and Josh's sister, Chloe."

"Are you going to have more?"

"I'm not sure. In some ways it might be nice to keep it small."

"Three's a nice number."

"That's what I thought." Of course, I don't mention that three sounds a little less expensive than, say, six.

"Have you decided yet on colors or anything?" she asks as she gets more hot water for her tea.

"I have some ideas. I was thinking since it's in June, maybe something in a pastel. Maybe pink or yellow or blue. Although I feel bad picking a color that you guys might not like. Pink satin probably isn't something you could ever wear again, and I've read how they're designing bridesmaid dresses that can be worn more than once."

"That's a big myth." Jenny rolls her eyes. "I've been in three weddings so far, and despite all that bunk about reusing the dresses, I know I'll never wear a single one of them again." She dips her tea bag and seems to consider this. "In fact, if I were you, I'd just choose dresses that are classy but not too expensive. Then go for really good shoes."

"I like the classy but not expensive idea," I tell her.

"And don't forget that bridesmaids cover their own clothing expenses."

"I know. But it seems unfair."

"Hey, it's the price you pay for being popular."

By the time Joy gets to the dorm, Jenny has already

given me lots of ideas. For one thing, she reminds me that all of my bridesmaids, so far, are brunettes. "You'll be like the fair maiden," she says. "The golden princess."

"But I should try to pick out a color that will look good on brunettes," I'm telling her as Josh's mom pulls up in her BMW.

I open the passenger door. "Do you mind if Jenny comes along?"

Joy smiles, but I can't tell if it's sincere or not. "Jenny Lambert, is that you?"

"It is indeed," says Jenny.

"The more the merrier," Joy says as she waits for us to get in.

"Jenny has such good taste," I say quickly. "And she's going to be a bridesmaid."

"Oh, good," says Joy. "Maybe she'll find something that will work for the bridesmaids today."

Suddenly I feel like betrayer times two. Not only have I left my mother out of this loop, but Beanie as well. And Beanie, of all people, is the real fashion expert. But here's the truth, and it's hard to admit—but Beanie's taste is just a little too extreme for me sometimes. I mean, she certainly has dramatic flair and a real sense of style and all that. But sometimes her suggestions feel more Beanie than Caitlin. And this is my wedding, and I want it to feel like it reflects who I am. Still, Beanie did come through on helping Josh pick out the perfect ring. Maybe I should give her a chance. Even so, there's nothing to be done about it today.

We go to a few shops before lunch, but I can tell that Jenny is getting tired. I suggest we take a break. "My head is starting to spin. If I see another wedding dress, I might faint."

Joy picks a restaurant in the mall, and after we're seated, Jenny points out a pasta dish that looks good to me.

"Oh, look," says Joy. "They have a low-carb section."

"Are you doing that diet?" asks Jenny.

Joy smiles. "Yes. I'm trying to shed a few pounds before the wedding."

I toss Jenny a glance, as if to warn her to stick with the pasta. "Well, Jenny doesn't <u>need</u> to lose any weight."

Joy nods. "I don't know how you do it, Jenny. Always just as thin as a supermodel."

I know Joy means this as a compliment, but it makes me want to throw something. Instead I say, "Jenny's lucky that way. She must have a really high metabolism, because she can put away that pasta and still look great." Of course, Jenny gives me a little kick under the table. "On the other hand, I'm trying to lose some weight. Maybe I should look into the low-carb diet."

"That's a great idea, Caitlin." Joy points to some kind of salad. "Maybe you should try this."

And so I don't argue with her, and feeling like I'm about seven years old, I actually let her order what turns out to be little more than a side salad for me. Okay, I fully realize that I've totally wimped out, but maybe it's worth it to keep everyone happy. And thankfully, Jenny orders the pasta. But after I polish off my salad and resist the bread, since Joy says it's full of carbs, I now find myself longing for some of Jenny's creamy-looking pasta. And believe me, nothing spoils a lunch quicker than food lust. But I try to control my feelings and am relieved that the conversation flows pleasantly. Mostly due to Jenny.

I feel slightly surprised at how easily Jenny converses with Joy. It's as if they're old friends. And while I know that Jenny and Josh dated for a while, I don't see how she and Josh's mom could've gotten this well acquainted, but it seems they did. Then I remember what Jenny said about Joy being just like her own mother. Of course, Jenny is used to this sort of thing. And really, I should be thankful. It allows me to relax a bit and even daydream.

"I think Vera Wang is the best," says Joy and Jenny nods.

"Or Bill Levkoff," adds Jenny. "He's very classic and more affordable."

"Yes, but if money were no object, I think a Wang would be perfect for Caitlin."

"I hear there are some good imitations that look exactly like the real thing," says Jenny. "But you have to know who to go through."

"A Vera Wang knockoff?" Joy seems to be considering this.

"Or a Levkoff knockoff," says Jenny, which makes them both laugh. And suddenly I wonder what on earth they're talking about. It's as if they're speaking another language—maybe wedding-ese.

Because we knew we'd be trying on dresses, Jenny made sure that we both wore outfits that would come off and on easily, as well as high-heeled shoes. But by midafternoon, my feet are killing me, and I am so done with this little shopping excursion. But unfortunately for me, Jenny has gotten her second wind (must be that pasta), and Joy seems unstoppable.

"How about this one?" Joy says as she holds up a satin number that doesn't look any different from at least a dozen others I've already tried on today. However, I know what will happen if I mention this fact. Both Joy and Jenny will point out the subtle details and differences in the cut or the skirt width or the train or the bodice or the whatever. Big deal. They all look like a bunch of long white satin dresses to me.

And I know that I'll be seeing these same dresses in my dreams tonight. It's all I can see when I close my eyes now. I'm sure I'll be haunted by white satin for days, maybe weeks, to come. Even so, I give in to peer pressure and go into the dressing room to try on the dress. Once again, and despite my mother's earlier reservations, this is another strapless number. And here's what's weird: Either these two are wearing me down, or I'm actually beginning to like this style.

Jenny fastens up the back of the dress, then I step out and do the obligatory walk, slowly and gracefully, as if I'm coming down the aisle. I give a half turn so they

can see the back, turn around to face them, and just
for fun I even curtsy.

"That's beautiful," says Joy, clapping her hands
together.

"It really is." Jenny turns me around to face the big
three-way mirror so I can see for myself.

I nod and consider the dress. It really is one of the
best ones I've seen, and it does fit me perfectly. Okay,
it's a little snug, but then I'm going to lose some weight by
June.

"I think we should get it," says Joy suddenly.

"Oh, I don't think—"

"She might be right, Cate. It looks fantastic on you.
Really. It's so perfect. It's by far the best one we've seen
all day."

"But I'm not really ready to—"

"When is the wedding?" asks the older woman who's
been helping us.

"June," offers Joy.

"It's not too soon to make a decision," says the woman.
"Some women get their dresses a year in advance. And
already we're getting backlogged on certain styles." She
peers at the dress I'm wearing. "Including this one." She
glances around, as if to see if anyone else is listening.
"And if you hadn't noticed, this dress is quite similar to a
Vera Wang that sells for thirteen thousand."

"No," Joy says, as if she'd just been told the dress
had been woven from gold thread spun by a traveling
band of leprechauns.

"Yes," says the saleswoman.

"I thought it looked familiar." Jenny examines the dress more closely.

"I don't expect we'll have this dress for long," says the saleswoman.

Now I'm feeling desperate. Like there's no way I can agree to buy this dress without both my mother's and Beanie's approval. This shopping trip has gotten totally out of control. I consider calling Josh on my cell phone, then wonder what he can possibly say.

"I really think you need to seriously consider this dress," says Joy.

I look at my reflection again. And okay, I'll admit it looks good. Really good. But even so, it feels wrong. "But I plan on losing some weight," I try using this as an excuse but know it probably sounds lame. "I mean, by June I could be a whole dress size smaller."

The saleswoman nods as if this makes perfect sense. "That's not unusual, dear. We never do the final alteration until a couple of weeks before the wedding. We want the dress to fit perfectly."

"But I—"

"No buts," says Joy. "I think this is the one, and I think we all know it."

"But I can't possibly buy it today." Then it occurs to me that it may be too expensive. "I don't even know how much it is." Joy told me earlier today not to even look at the prices. "Just try things on," she said. "See how they feel and what you like." So I have totally disregarded price tags.

The saleswoman looks at the tag in the back of my dress, then finally says, "It's only nineteen nine."

"Ninety-nine?" I repeat, incredulous at the bargain. I turn and look at the dress again. "Really, did I hear you right? Did you say ninety-nine dollars?"

She smiles and looks slightly embarrassed for me. "Nineteen hundred and nine dollars."

Jenny laughs. "Oh, you knew that, Cate."

"Yeah, sure," I say, but at least Jenny understands. And I do know this: That is only ninety-one dollars less than two thousand. And there is no way I will let my parents pay that kind of money for a dress I will only wear once.

"That's not so bad," says Joy. "Some of the dresses you tried on today were three times that."

"No way," I say and instantly regret it. It's as if I'm trying to look like the country bumpkin today. But I am just plain tired. And I am sick and tired of trying on stupid, expensive dresses.

"How about if I put it on my card?" says Joy. "You can take it home, show your parents, and see if they don't absolutely love it."

"Oh, no, I can't let you—"

"I insist." She turns to the clerk now. "If her parents don't agree, is this returnable?"

"Certainly." The woman smiles as if this sale is in the

bag. "As long as no damage is done to the dress."

"But I can't—"

"No, Caitlin," says Joy. "You need to give this dress a chance. If you don't get it today, it could be gone by the time you come to your senses and realize that it's perfect for you."

I turn to Jenny for some moral support, but she is just nodding. "Really, you look like royalty in that."

"She has sort of a Princess Grace look, doesn't she?" says the saleswoman.

"I think you're right," says Joy. "I just loved the old Grace Kelly movies."

I don't even know who they're talking about, but it seems like I'm not even in the room anyway. I return to the dressing room where Jenny helps me to remove the gown. "This is crazy," I tell her.

"You look amazing in that dress," Jenny says in a slightly irritated voice. "I would kill to look that gorgeous, and you act like you can't even see it."

I pause and study her to see if she's just stringing me along. "Really? You think it's that great?"

"Maybe it's like me and anorexia," she says as she reverently arranges the ribbons that hold the dress in place on the hanger. "It's like we can't really see ourselves."

And that just gets to me. So I allow Josh's mother to put the dress on her credit card, but the whole time I'm thinking this is all wrong.

I sit in silence as Joy drives us back to our dorm. It

doesn't really matter since she and Jenny are chatting congenially, just like old friends. And while I feel the slightest bit jealous over the way Josh's old girlfriend is suddenly bonding with my mother-in-law to be, I am also thankful because I'm so worn out that I can think of nothing to say.

By the time we reach the dorm, it is agreed, and I must admit wisely so (although I had nothing to do with it personally), that the dress should remain with Joy until I come home and have a chance to try it on for my parents.

"That way we can be sure that it will be in perfect condition, in the unlikely event you decide not to go with it."

"But you won't do that," Jenny says with the kind of confidence I'll probably never have when it comes to things of fashion or big price tags.

"That's right," agrees Joy. "You won't do that."

The two of them laugh about this, then Jenny and I climb out, and after thanking Joy, we wave good-bye.

"I feel like I've been through the wedding wringer today," I admit as we trudge up the stairs.

"I think we should order a pizza up to our room," suggests Jenny.

I turn and look at her and wonder if this is really Jenny. "Seriously?"

She kind of laughs. "Yeah, all this shopping makes me hungry."

So our pizza comes, and we get out all of the brides'

magazines. We spread them all over the floor and study the styles of bridesmaid dresses that would best go with the dress that's riding home in the trunk of Josh's mother's BMW.

It's not until Jenny has gone to sleep and I'm recording all this into my diary that I know I have made a big mistake. But I'm so tired I can't even totally remember how it happened. And there is no way I can figure out how I'm going to undo it. So I just pray.

DEAR GOD, I KNOW I'VE BLOWN IT. I KNOW I FAILED TO HEED THAT STILL, SMALL VOICE THAT WAS SCREAMING ITS HEAD OFF INSIDE OF ME— EMPHATICALLY TELLING ME NOT TO GET THAT STUPID DRESS. BUT LIKE A FOOL, I WASN'T LISTENING. AND NOW I KNOW IT'S GOING TO BE A GREAT, BIG MESS TO UNRAVEL THIS WHOLE CRAZY DRESS BUSINESS. I KNOW THAT FEELINGS WILL PROBABLY GET HURT, AND IT WILL BE MY OWN FAULT. I JUST PRAY FOR YOUR MERCY AND GRACE AND THAT YOU WILL HELP ME. AND PLEASE, I BEG YOU, PLEASE, HELP ME NOT TO BE SO EASILY SUCKED IN NEXT TIME. I'M REALLY SORRY. AMEN.

SEVEN

Sunday, November 6

I feel slightly depressed as Jenny and I walk over to the church service. Fortunately, she doesn't even seem to notice as she talks about a bridesmaid dress that she discovered in one of my magazines this morning.

"It's so perfect," she tells me. "Very sleek and classic, and it's actually from Macy's, so it might not be too expensive."

I listen as she goes back and forth about the color, trying to decide why lilac or yellow might work better than pink. And I try to respond as if I'm paying attention, but all I can think is that I made a big mistake yesterday by allowing Josh's mother to purchase that dress.

The sermon in church is actually pretty good, and I find I'm feeling a little better as we walk back to the dorm, except that it's starting to rain.

"What a dreary day," Jenny says as she pulls her scarf over her head.

"A good day to just stay inside and catch up on homework."

"Or sleep."

And so after some lunch at the deli, that's exactly what we do. But later in the afternoon, the ringing of the phone wakes me from my nap. It turns out to be Josh, and he sounds very happy.

"The workathon was a huge success," he tells me after we've made our significant small talk about missing each other and how long it's going to be until next weekend.

"What happened? How did it go?"

"It was great. It's like it couldn't have gone any better. I was surprised when practically everyone in the youth group showed up. They'd all gotten lots of sponsors to pay so much per hour. And by the time we quit, almost everyone had worked about twenty hours total."

"You must be tired."

"It was really fun though. I'd put up some posters at the senior center and a couple of grocery stores. And you should've seen how many people signed up. Of course, who turns down free labor? Mostly, we did yard work for elderly and shut-ins, things like raking leaves, cleaning gutters, taking down screens. But the kids were awesome."

"That's so cool, Josh."

"And then we treated the kids to a pizza party at the church, and I sort of calculated how much money we'd raised, you know, once the pledges come in. I couldn't believe that it was nearly two thousand dollars! I did some quick mental math, and based on the average number of kids at the dump, we made enough money to feed them for most of the winter. Can you believe that? Well, the kids thought it was pretty cool."

"That's awesome."

We talk some more, and since Josh was enjoying such a high about his successful fund-raiser, I didn't have the heart to tell him about the disappointing shopping day I'd had with his mother. I knew it could wait. Or maybe I could even e-mail him about it later.

It was only after I hung up that it occurred to me that the same amount of money these high school kids raised—enough to feed ten to fifteen starving Mexican children for several months—was about the same cost as the wedding dress I'd been talked into purchasing yesterday. And the idea of this just made me feel sick.

Jenny is still asleep and I decide to take a walk since the weather had cleared slightly. And as I walk, I pray. I ask for God to guide me through this whole wedding thing. More than anything, I want our wedding to honor God. And I know that my actions yesterday were not heading in that direction.

It's funny too, because I'm not the kind of girl who everyone can push around so easily. I mean, I'll admit that I like to make people happy and I sometimes try too hard to help others. But I don't usually compromise my own standards or convictions along the way. Still, I can see how it will be challenging with Josh's mom. She's such a strong and persuasive person. A little like a steamroller. I guess I just need to learn to stand up to her. Not aggressively, but kindly and in love.

Finally, I come to my favorite thinking and praying bench, and although it's still wet, I sit down. The sermon at church today was about laying things down on God's altar. The Scripture was from the time when Abraham had to take Isaac up to the mountain as a sacrifice. Now I'm familiar with this story, and it's not the first time I've had to put something on God's altar. In fact, there was a time when I had to place Josh there. But today I know, as clearly as I know my own name, that I need to place our wedding on God's altar. I need to give all my hopes and dreams and expectations to God. I need to lay the perfect dress and location and reception and music and invitations and decorations...all on God's altar.

I sit there for a long time, with the dampness from the bench soaking right into my jeans, and I imagine myself doing just this. I see myself placing the whole bundle of satin and lace and roses and pastel colors and veils and shoes all on the altar. And then I lift up the knife and I kill them. God doesn't even send in an alternative sacrifice (like he did for Abraham) to stop me. I just kill them.

The funny thing is that I feel better when these wedding dreams are dead. I don't care if there's blood all over the white satin. It's just a huge relief. And as I stand up and thank God for this revelation, I imagine

myself wearing a gunnysack dress and carrying a dan-
delion bouquet as I walk down the aisle toward Josh. And
I am perfectly fine with this. All that I want is God's will.

I call the Miller house on my cell phone then. I'm
ready to tell Joy that as much as I appreciate her help
and input, I know without a doubt that the dress needs
to be returned. Period. No discussion. I will apologize for
the inconvenience and even explain how I want this wedding to be God directed. But I will be firm.

To my surprise Josh answers. "It's you."

He laughs. "Caitlin?"

"Yes, I'm sorry. I guess I expected your mom to answer."

"Oh." He sounds disappointed now, and I feel bad.

"Not that I don't want to talk to you."

"Oh, good. The parents are out at the moment."

"It's just that I needed to talk to your mom."

"Is something wrong?"

"Sort of." And so I tell him the humiliating story of how
I was a total pushover yesterday. I even tell him about
lunch, and how I was hungry after grazing on greens.
"That probably didn't help anything."

Of course, he's laughing now. "Poor Caitie. But good
grief, girl. What is wrong with you? You do NOT need to
lose any weight. You are absolutely perfect the way you
are."

"Really?"

"Would I lie to you?"

"But what if I feel like I need to get into better
shape for myself?"

"There's nothing wrong with getting into shape. But if you think you need to get all skinny as a stick for our wedding, well, forget about it. What you girls don't realize is that most guys like a little meat on their women."

"Sounds like you're hungry."

He laughs. "Maybe I am. But seriously, Caitlin. I don't go for skinny chicks. Most guys don't."

"Are you saying I'm chubby?"

"Not at all. If anything, I think you're on the thin side, and I wouldn't care if you put on weight."

"Well, I don't really plan to—"

"Believe me, I think you're perfect. I love you just the way you are, and I think I'd love you just as much if you weighed two hundred pounds."

"Oh, come on."

"Really. I love you. That's the way it is."

"Thanks, Josh. I love you too. And if you end up fat and bald and I am wrinkled and gray, we'll still love each other. Right?"

"Right."

"But back to the dress dilemma," I say. "I want to get it resolved as soon as possible."

"I don't blame you."

Then I tell him about how depressed I was to consider how the cost of that stupid dress was equal to what his youth group had earned.

"That's because your heart's in the right place," he assures me. "But obviously, you just got caught up in the moment. And believe me, I know how persuasive my mom can be. You should've heard Chloe and her going at it a few years ago. Fortunately for Chloe, they seem to have reached some understanding. But it seems like she's putting you into that daughter role now."

"Maybe so."

"And planning for our wedding shouldn't make you miserable, Caitlin."

"I know." And then I explain about what I've just done, how I've placed our wedding on the altar and slit its pretty satin throat. "There was blood everywhere."

"It's a great image," he says with enthusiasm. "I love it." And then I know he totally gets me. I am so glad that I'm marrying someone who gets me.

"I felt so relieved," I continue. "It's like this huge weight was lifted."

"Cool."

"Oh, I know there'll still be some challenges, but I feel like I'm ready for it. I think I can even stand up to your mom."

"You go, girl!"

"And I feel like I know what's really important now."

"Like our marriage?"

"Yes. I mean, a wedding is a great way for people to celebrate, but it really shouldn't take over your life."

"I agree."

"So we're united?"

"You bet."

"When do you think your mom will be back?"

"I don't know, but I can have her call you. Will you be back in your dorm then?"

"Yeah."

"Do you mind if I talk to her first? I'd like to explain that I'm totally with you on this. I want her to see that we're united."

"That's great, Josh. I'd appreciate it."

"Oh, yeah," he says. "One more thing. Can you handle another piece of bad news as far as wedding plans?"

I kind of laugh. "Hey, it's on the altar, remember?"

"Yeah. God's in control, right?"

"Right."

"Well, Saint Matthew's is booked on the day you gave me."

"That's okay, something will work out."

And really, I'm not worried. God has this whole wedding thing under control. Not only that, but when Joy calls at around eight, our conversation goes surprisingly smoothly. She says she talked to Josh, that he explained everything, and that she understands. Of course, she adds that she was a bit disappointed to let the <u>perfect</u> dress get away.

"I know it was beautiful," I admit to her. "But it wasn't perfect. That's too much money for me to feel comfortable with. And I know that God has something even better for me."

"You kids. I don't know where you get that kind of faith."

I kind of laugh now. "From God."

"Yes, that's what Chloe and Josh tell me too. I guess I'm just a little slow on the uptake."

"Hey, as long as you're on the uptake," I say. "That's what matters."

"You're a good girl, Caitlin."

I thank her and tell her I love her and then hang up.

"So that's it for the dress?" says Jenny, looking up from her laptop.

"Yeah." Then I tell her about my revelation on the bench. And to my relief, she seems to respect this.

"That'd be hard though," she says. "I mean, most girls have certain expectations about their wedding day. I don't know if I could give all that up."

"You could if you believed God had something better for you."

She nods and turns back to her computer. "Yeah, maybe so."

DEAR GOD, THANKS FOR MEETING ME ON THE BENCH TODAY. YOU ARE SO AWESOME! THANK YOU FOR SETTING ME STRAIGHT ABOUT MY WEDDING. AND HELP ME TO KEEP GIVING IT ALL BACK TO YOU. I AM SO RELIEVED NOT TO BE CARRYING THAT WEIGHT ANYMORE. YOU LOVE ME SO MUCH, GOD! THANK YOU! THANK YOU! THANK YOU! AMEN.

EIGHT

Wednesday, November 16

So far so good with our little nightly weigh-in plan. Jenny has put on a whole two pounds, although I still weigh the same. But I attribute this to the fact that I'm now doing Pilates and muscle weighs more than fat. At least that's what Liz told me when she loaned me her Pilates video. And since I've been doing them every night, I think I've actually turned some fat into muscle. Jenny works out with me. At first she got tired after only a few minutes, but she's increasing her endurance.

Mostly, I'm just relieved that she's still eating. Okay, she's not exactly a porker, but she's eating a lot more than before. And even though I haven't lost any weight yet, I can already tell that my stomach is firmer. I feel hopeful.

Since last weekend, I have barely given the wedding a thought. It's like I know everything's going to work out just fine. Even so, I'm bracing myself for the upcoming weekend. I'm sure that between Josh's mother and mine, there will be some new development or questions. But I am ready.

Sunday, November 20

To my amazement, the weekend went smoothly and uneventfully. I guess everyone is consumed with Thanksgiving plans at the moment. Kind of a wedding planning reprieve for me. And next will be Christmas. Maybe I'll be able to finish fall term without too much pressure.

Josh and I had lunch with Chloe, Allie, and Laura on Saturday. The girls are getting ready to go out on a holiday tour. You could really see the excitement in their eyes.

"You make me wish that I was going," I told them. "It sounds like it's going to be great."

"We wish you were going too," said Allie.

"How are the newlyweds doing?" I asked.

"All right." Allie nodded. "Sounded like they had an awesome time on their honeymoon. My mom even went parasailing." She laughed. "Can you believe that?"

"Good for her," said Josh. "Maybe we'll have to do something like that on our honeymoon." He winked at me from across the table.

"Do you guys know where you're going yet?" asked Laura.

"Maybe Mexico. Caitlin and I plan to spend our summer at the mission."

Chloe frowned. "If you're spending the whole summer down there, maybe you should go someplace different for your honeymoon."

"Maybe." Josh considered this. "Well, there's plenty of time to figure it all out."

And then I decided to tell these girls about how I'd put our wedding on God's altar. I know these girls well enough to know that they'll get it. And they totally did.

"That is so cool, Caitlin," said Chloe.

"Yeah," agreed Allie. "You're such a great role model for us."

I had to laugh about that. Then I confessed to them about how just the day before I'd made such a total mess of things. I mean, I don't want these girls thinking I'm something I'm not. "It's a learning thing," I finally said.

"Life's like that," said Chloe.

She's right. Life is like that. But without God it would be learning through the school of hard knocks on a daily basis. I've seen others doing it that way, and I feel sorry for them. Not that I think my life should be pain-free and smooth (and it's not), but I don't mind getting directions from God. If He sees a Mack truck about to plow me down, I don't mind Him telling me to take a little detour now and then. Besides, the scenery is usually better anyway.

DEAR GOD, THANKS FOR GIVING ME PEACE IN MY
LIFE. I KNOW THAT IT WON'T ALWAYS BE LIKE
THIS, BUT I DO ENJOY THESE TIMES WHEN I CAN
JUST REST IN YOU AND KNOW THAT YOU'RE
LEADING AND GUIDING ME. AND ONCE AGAIN, I
COMMIT MY WAY TO YOU. AMEN.

Friday, November 25

Wow, what a busy last few days it's been. Josh picked me
up at school on Wednesday night, and then we split our
Thanksgiving Day between his family and mine.

"Better get used to this," warned my mom. "Once you
get married, the holidays get tricky." She shook her
head. "And it's even worse after the kids come." Then
she smiled. "Not that I don't want grandkids, sweetie. I
do."

I laughed. "Well, don't hold your breath. Both Josh
and I agree that we don't plan on having children for at
least five years. Our kids will be the ones down in
Mexico."

Of course, this made my mom look sad, and I wished I
hadn't said it. Still, it's the truth. Josh and I are both
committed to doing whatever we can for all the orphans
in the world. We're not absolutely sure this will put us in
Mexico for the rest of our lives, but we're open to the possibility. We just want what God wants. And we have to
trust that our parents will be okay with this, eventually.

So Thanksgiving seemed to go well, and it was fun

meeting some of Josh's extended family. I especially liked Grandma Brown. She is a very down-to-earth woman and quite different from her daughter Joy. Naturally, I didn't mention this, but I think Grandma Brown sensed that I felt a special connection with her.

"Bring Caitlin down to the farm sometimes," Grandma Brown said as we were leaving to head back over to my parents' for dessert and charades.

Josh nodded and I told her I'd love it. And I would.

Then we got to spend the rest of the evening with my family. Tony and Steph and the boys were there, as well as my grandma who's getting ready to head down to Arizona next week.

"How long are you going to be gone this time?" I asked her.

"Maybe March or April." She grinned. "But don't worry, I'll be back in time for all the wedding festivities. Your mother promised to keep me informed."

"I know Marigold died last year," I said, "But are you still going to have a house sitter?"

She frowned. "I don't have anyone lined up to stay there, now that I don't have the cat to think about, but Stephie has offered to water my plants."

"Yeah, I can't wait." Aunt Steph rolled her eyes at me when Grandma was not looking. Now, my grandma has about a hundred plants. Really, her house is like a jungle. Even so, I like it.

"Hey, I could stay at your house on weekends," I suggested. "I know how to water your plants."

My grandma brightened. "You'd do that for me, honey?"

"Sure. And then Mom can have her craft room back."

"Oh, you don't need to worry about that," said my mom.

"But what about the wedding preparations?" I reminded her, trying not to imagine what those awful crepe-paper flowers would look like. "Didn't you want to use that room to get some things ready?"

"That would be nice."

"And it would be nice if Caitlin could keep an eye on things for me," said Grandma.

"It would be nice if I didn't have to spend half a day watering Mom's plants," added Aunt Steph.

So it was settled. I will become the weekend occupant of Grandma's house until she comes back next spring. Already I was thinking about Christmas break and how cool it would be to have Beanie and Jenny over to visit me. This is going to be awesome!

DEAR GOD, THANKS FOR YOUR GREAT PLANS FOR ME. IT'S AS IF YOU'RE WALKING AHEAD OF ME AND JUST GETTING THINGS READY. HELP ME TO KEEP MY EYES ON YOU AND TO OBEY YOU. HELP MY LIFE TO BE A REFLECTION OF YOUR LOVE. AMEN.

Saturday, November 26

Just when I thought life was as good as it can get—I mean, being engaged to the greatest guy and relaxing at home and spending time with my family—well, then it gets even better. Chloe had invited me over to her house tonight. "Just to see you one more time before we leave on tour," she'd told me on the phone. Josh picked me up around seven, then stopped off at the store to pick up some ice cream for Chloe. When we got to the Miller house, there were cars everywhere.

"Looks like a party," I said as we walked up to the door.

"Maybe a send-off for the girls," said Josh. "Although no one mentioned anything."

As soon as we got through the door, everyone yelled SURPRISE! There in Josh's living room were lots of our old friends from high school, friends from church, and family members. And it turned out that this was an engagement party, hosted by none other that Miss Chloe Miller (rock star and wonder girl). And believe me, she'd gone to great expense (secretly hiring a caterer) to bring in the best our town has to offer. It was awesome.

But even better than the food was visiting with old friends and catching up on what was going on in their lives. Really, I can't imagine having more fun. Even Anna and Joel Johnson were there. Anna pulled me aside and congratulated me.

"You guys are doing this right," she said in a happy voice, but her eyes looked sad.

"Thanks."

"I wish we'd done it this way too."

Now I knew that life had been tough for Anna and

Joel. Although they were both Christians, they chose to sleep together in their first year in college. And not long after that, Anna got pregnant.

After they were married, Anna dropped out of school so she could work to help support them. But Joel had to get a part-time job, and Beanie told me that their marriage got a little rocky. To be honest, I was pleasantly surprised tonight to see they were still together. And then Anna showed me pictures of their little girl Hannah when she had just turned two. She's a doll with Anna's big brown eyes and skin the color of cocoa. Really beautiful.

"So it's going well for you," I said, feeling relieved.

"It's still hard. Joel has another year before he graduates, and that's if everything goes well and I can keep on working."

"Is there any reason you can't?" I asked.

She shook her head. "I haven't told anyone, but I'm afraid that I'm pregnant again." And then she burst into tears, and we had to go into the guest bedroom to avoid being overheard.

"But you guys made it through the first baby," I told her. "Maybe this won't be so hard this time. And Joel only has a year until he graduates." I was trying to be positive as I hugged her and listened to her cry.

"I know. But Joel's going to be so discouraged. It's expensive having one child in day care, and my job pays so little." She stepped back and shook her head. "Really, Caitlin, you've done this thing right. I wish I'd waited too."

"All you can do is take it from here," I told her. "Joel's a great guy, and you are an intelligent and capable woman. You guys will get through this, Anna. I just know it. And if nothing else, maybe you can use your story to help others make better choices. Is Joel still heading into the ministry?"

"He wants to."

"He's always been such a gifted speaker."

"It just seems to take so long. I mean, he's taken heavy class loads and works like a dog, but it's so hard to get ahead like this."

"But there's an end in sight," I remind her. "And more than that, God can get you through this. You know that."

She nodded. "I do know that. It just doesn't feel like it at the moment."

"When are you due? I mean, if it's the real thing and you're really pregnant."

"The middle of June."

I frowned. "So you probably don't want to be in my wedding then."

She shook her head. "You know I'd love to. And in a different life I would leap at the opportunity. But I just can't commit to that."

"But you will come?"

"If I'm not in labor."

"You're going to be okay, Anna. Better than okay. I really believe that God is going to do something amazing with you and Joel. I mean, look at my Aunt Steph. You should've seen her life about six years ago. Unwed mother, wild woman. Seriously, we all thought she was a total mess."

"Really?" Anna looked shocked. "Now she's a pastor's wife and more together than most people."

"See? If you let Him, God can do anything."

"Thanks, Caitlin."

But I still feel badly for Anna and Joel. Oh, I definitely believe what I told her in the guest bedroom. But I know they still have some bumps in the road ahead. Not that we all don't have bumps ahead. But I noticed the way Joel was talking to his old friends, getting excited about seeing them. It's like he was totally ignoring Anna. Almost as if he was ashamed of her. And well, that just got to me.

Still, it's not my place to judge. And who knows what those two have been through already. I agree with the old "unless you've walked a mile in their shoes" adage. Even so, I'm really glad that Josh and I have built a different kind of foundation for our relationship. And I hope that with God's help, we can keep it this sturdy and strong for the rest of our years together.

DEAR GOD, THANKS FOR ALL YOU'VE DONE TO
KEEP MY LIFE ON TRACK. THANKS FOR LEADING ME
EVEN NOW. PLEASE, GOD, HELP ANNA AND JOEL TO
MAKE IT THROUGH THE NEXT YEAR. HELP THEM
TO LEAN ON YOU, AND TURN THEIR WEAKNESSES
INTO YOUR STRENGTHS. HELP THEM TO ADMIT
WHEN THEY'VE BLOWN IT, AND USE THEIR PAST
MISTAKES TO MAKE THEM WISER IN THE FUTURE.
MOST OF ALL, PLEASE, HELP THEM TO MAKE GOOD
CHOICES RIGHT NOW AND TO HONOR YOU WITH
THEIR LIVES AND THEIR MARRIAGE. AND PLEASE,
BLESS THEIR CHILDREN! AMEN.

NINE

Last weekend I felt like I was on top of the world. This week I feel like I'm drowning in the pits. Go figure. But then life is like that. I think it's just God's way of reminding us that we're not so hot. Still, I could've gotten along fine without this.

Okay, never mind that this is dead week (next week is finals), and that's bad enough. But as I'm cramming for finals and trying to fight off a cold, I have a problem that's eating me alive. I guess I should've been prepared for this. But I was so caught up in the la-la land of engagement and being in love that I just missed it. Or maybe I was in big fat denial. Maybe I am the Queen of Denial. Even now, I wonder why I am bothering to write about this in my diary. I mean, I still should be studying. But then it feels like I'm going to burst if I don't get this out. So here goes nothing.

After a blissful weekend at home and the wonderful

party Chloe hosted, I really thought life was good. But maybe that's as good as it gets. Maybe it's going to be downhill from here. Oh, I hope not!

It all started on Sunday afternoon. At the engagement party the night before, Jenny had asked to bum a ride back to school with Josh and me. Her parents had just left town for a couple of days in Las Vegas, and Jenny was stuck without a ride. Of course, we said that was fine.

Then as we were riding, we were talking about seeing our old friends again and how it was almost like a reunion, and then we started reminiscing about old high school days. It was actually pretty fun.

"Yeah, I remember when we first started getting to know each other, Cate," Jenny said from the backseat. "You'd been kind of this wallflower chick."

"I wasn't exactly a wallflower," I protested. "Okay, maybe a little shy. But Beanie and I didn't really fit in with all you popular kids. You guys were too intimidating for us."

She laughed. "Little did you know."

"Yeah," said Josh. "We popular kids were probably the ones who were most intimidated."

"How's that?" I asked.

"Well, we had to keep up, you know? Never let your guard down. Always stay on top and in control. It was hard."

"That's right," agreed Jenny. "A real dog-eat-dog world."

"Yeah," said Josh. "Lonely at the top."

"Oh, puleeze." I laughed. But then I knew they were sort of right. I'd been in the popular crowd briefly, and it was one of the worst times of my life.

"Luckily, we all survived." Josh turned and grinned at me.

"And look at you two now," said Jenny. "I mean, who would've thought, way back then, that you guys would get married someday?"

"Oh, I don't know," I said. "I'd had my eye on Josh for a long time."

"Really?" asked Josh. "When did you first start liking me?"

I laughed. "Seriously?"

"Yeah, tell me. When did you first notice me?"

"Back in my freshman year. We had biology together. You sat in front of me, and I would sit there and daydream about you."

"Really? Way back then?"

"Pathetic, huh?"

"No, not at all. I think it's sweet."

"Okay then, when did you first notice me?" I asked.

"To be honest?"

"Yes," I said in a firm voice. "Honesty would be nice."

"Well, it was probably that drinking party when I walked into the den and saw you sitting all by yourself in that big leather chair." He laughed. "You were so cute."

"I remember that," said Jenny. "And if memory serves

me right, you and I were still going together then."

"I think we'd broken up by then."

"That's right," I said suddenly. "When we were working on decorations for the Valentine's dance, I remember you telling me what a jerk he was."

"You actually remember that?" Jenny sounded surprised.

"Yeah, that was kind of a turning point in my life," I admitted. "I was just breaking into the cool crowd then."

"Oh, yeah." Jenny laughed. "And that's when you moved in on my boyfriend."

I turned around and looked at her. "Are you serious? Did you really think I moved in on Josh?"

She laughed even harder. "No, I'm just messing with you, Cate. Actually, as I recall, it was kind of a comedy of errors. We were both chasing after the same guy, and he really knew how to play us."

Josh looked sad. "I was such a jerk."

"That's right," said Jenny.

"That's right," I agreed.

And then we started talking about something else. But that little conversation got me to thinking. And suddenly, as if someone flicked some kind of old rerun movie on, I began to remember some of the things that happened that year. Things I think I've worked very hard to forget.

In all fairness, I think I'd worked hard to forget them because they involved forgiveness issues. I mean, Jenny and I eventually became very good friends, and I couldn't very well go around holding a grudge against her or recalling every single thing she'd done to hurt me. Mostly with Josh. And then Josh and I started going out and getting serious, and it wasn't fair for me to hold things against him that had happened with Jenny. Forgive and forget, right? Move on. And so I did.

In time those memories just faded, and it was like those things never even happened. Until Sunday afternoon.

After we arrived at the dorm, Jenny went inside. (I'm sure to give us privacy to say good night, which we did with several very nice kisses.) And then I went inside and started doing some last-minute tweaking on a paper that was due the next day. Jenny was working too.

And then we did our little weigh-in routine. (And despite eating like a pig over the weekend, I had actually lost a pound and Jenny had gained one, so we were happy.) And then we went to bed. But instead of going to sleep, I started being haunted by high school memories. Most of all by the fact that my roommate and good friend Jenny Lambert had slept with my fiancé and true love Josh Miller. They had had sex.

Oh, I don't know why this had to be so disturbing just then. And in my defense I was having PMS. But it's as if someone just dumped a load of stinking crud on me, and all I could think of was that Josh had done IT with Jenny, that Jenny had done IT with Josh. And sheesh, what kind of fool am I to think they can't remember that? Why hadn't I remembered it myself? See what I mean? The Queen of Denial.

Well, since I'm the queen, I did a great job of commanding my royal feelings under the rug the next day. And the next. And the next. Oh, Jenny asked me a couple of times why I was so quiet, but I told her that I always get like this before finals. And since she's never roomed with me before, she bought it.

"You really take school seriously, don't you?"

I nodded as I looked up from my book. "Don't you?"

She shrugged. "Yeah, I guess."

Okay, here's the dilemma—do I bring this up with her? Do I tell her what's bugging me and try to talk it through, work it all out? In some ways I think that'd just be fruitlessly painful for both of us. Because despite my having suffered this convenient "amnesia" all these years, my memory has returned with crystal clarity now, and I specifically recall Jenny telling me that she lost her virginity to Josh during the spring of his senior year. It was her attempt to win him back (from me).

Little did she know that at the time, I'd already decided to break things off with him. And even though she gave him her virginity, he still broke up with her, still broke her heart, and I know he lost respect for her. If anything, her effort to keep Josh made him even more attracted to me. But I was done with him by then. And I was done with dating as well.

So what do I do now? I've considered calling Josh and telling him how I feel, but what good would it do? I mean, what happened nearly five years ago was between him and Jenny—and between him and God. I know God has forgiven Josh, and I'm pretty sure Jenny has too. I even thought I'd forgiven him—not to mention wiped my memory clean of it—but now it's like it's here again. Right in my face.

And it's not that I'm holding it against Jenny; I'm not. But it does feel awkward rooming with her and going through all this crud. I think it's about to make my head explode.

Finally, it occurred to me that I should call Beanie. I mean, what are best friends for? Besides that, she knows about Josh and Jenny's history; I won't even have to explain the whole thing to her. But unfortunately, Beanie hasn't been answering her phone today. I left a couple of desperate messages and e-mailed her as well.

And now I'm going to bed, feeling hopeless and confused all over again. Will this ever end? Have I made a mistake to agree to marry a guy with a past? Okay, I realize that by today's standards, it's not much of a past. And I know that Josh during his college years was committed to abstinence just like me. At least I think he was. But then I haven't exactly asked him. It's not as though it comes up in everyday conversation, like "Hey, Josh, did you ever have sex with anyone besides Jenny Lambert?" And now I'm thinking, what if he has? How would I feel? I already feel pretty rotten about this, and it's not even news to me.

So here's the thing: I know I'm not perfect. Believe me, I know I have LOTS of faults, have made LOTS of mistakes, and have LOTS of room to grow. But I've tried to obey God. I've kept my abstinence pledge to Him. I am still a virgin. So why am I the one suffering here? Trust me, Jenny is sleeping soundly right now. I'll bet that Josh is too. Tell me, why am I the one who's in pain?

And does this mean I've made a mistake? Does this mean that Josh really isn't the ONE for me? I feel so confused and upset. And if I don't get a handle on this thing, I may just end up blowing off my finals week. And then where will I be?

DEAR GOD, I REALLY NEED YOUR HELP ON THIS. I AM SO MIXED UP RIGHT NOW. AND MAYBE I'M BLOWING THIS WAY OUT OF PROPORTION, BUT I CAN'T DENY HOW I FEEL. RIGHT NOW I FEEL LIKE CRUD. AND SUDDENLY THE IDEA OF BEING ENGAGED AND PLANNING FOR A MARRIAGE FEELS DULL AND TAINTED. LIKE I DON'T EVEN WANT ANY PART OF IT. MAYBE JOSH WAS RIGHT ALL THOSE YEARS AGO WHEN HE ASKED ME IF I PLANNED TO BECOME A NUN. MAYBE I SHOULD BECOME A NUN. OKAY, I'M NOT EVEN CATHOLIC, BUT WE COULD WORK SOMETHING OUT. OH, GOD, I AM SO MISERABLE. PLEASE, HELP ME OUT OF THIS ABYSS. AMEN.

TEN

Saturday, December 3

In our weigh-in tonight, I discover I have lost a total of five pounds.

"Wow," says Jenny. "You're really doing great. But I hope you're not turning anorexic on me."

I shake my head. "No, it's just prefinals jitters and this stupid cold." Okay, it's a lie, but what am I going to say? "No, Jenny, it's just that I'm freaking out over the fact that you slept with my fiancé five years ago." Yeah, sure.

"Want to go out to celebrate?" she asks.

I look at the clock. "It's kind of late."

"Bryce and some of the kids from the fellowship group were meeting at Starbucks for a late night coffee."

"You go ahead and go if you want," I tell her. "I'm still feeling kind of crummy from this cold."

"You sure?"

"Yeah."

"Want me to bring you back something?"

"Nah. I'm okay." And so she leaves, but I am not okay. I'm pacing around this room like a caged animal that wants to tear into someone. And I nearly jump out of my skin when the phone rings. I grab it expecting it to be Josh but then remember he has high school fellowship group on Saturdays. To my huge relief, it's my best friend.

"Beanie!" I practically shriek into the receiver. "I can't believe it's you. Did you get all my messages?"

"Yeah, I'm so sorry I couldn't call sooner. Oh, Caitlin, this has been quite a week."

I can tell by her voice that something big has happened. For all I know she's met Mr. Wonderful and is getting married next month. "What?" I demand. "What's going on?"

"Don't you want to tell me your news first?" she says. "It sounded urgent."

"No, no, that's okay. It's not really news. I just wanted to talk. Now quit keeping me in suspense, Beanie. What's up?"

So then she launches into this story of how she's been trying to get into one of the big New York design schools and how suddenly not only one, but two of the best schools are interested in her. "My mom is paying for me to fly out after finals to interview with them. And there could be a scholarship involved. Oh, it's so amazing. I feel like Cinderella."

I am so happy for her that I temporarily forget about my troubles. "Oh, Beanie, if anyone deserves this kind of break, it's you. I've been praying for something like this."

"I'm so excited. I have my last final on Wednesday, and I fly out the next morning. Oh, I wish you could come."

"Me too." And I do; I really do. I would love to escape the torturing memories trying to ruin my life right now. Even if it was only briefly.

"I've got so much to do by then," she continues. "Besides finals, I have to polish up my portfolio, and then I need to put some fantastic-looking outfits together. I really need to wow these people. I mean, this is like the big times. Oh, I hope I don't end up looking like yesterday's news."

"You won't," I assure her. "You always end up looking like the hottest trendsetter around."

"But this is New York. Manhattan even."

"Just remember to breathe, Beanie."

"Yeah, good advice." And I hear her taking in a deep breath.

"And then remember that the God of the universe is your Daddy."

"Even better. So what's up with you? I barely got to talk to you at the engagement party. Man, what a spread that Chloe put together. She rocks."

"Chloe's amazing. You know that they're leaving tomorrow."

"Speaking of Chloe, do you know that designing for them is one of the things that really drew the attention of these schools? They both mentioned how that was quite an accomplishment for someone my age."

"I'm proud of you, Beanie."

"So really, Caitlin, tell me what's going on with you. What was so urgent that you left me three voice messages?"

I calmly tell her what's bugging me. I can't believe how even I keep my voice. I think I almost convince myself that it's really no big deal. "It's kind of silly, isn't it?" I finally say. "But for some reason it just really—"

"No, I don't think it's silly. To be honest, I wondered when you'd have to deal with this."

I couldn't respond to that.

"I mean, here you are rooming with Jenny, and I totally love her, you know that. But after you've made such a big deal of waiting, and now you're going to get married, but you know that Josh and Jenny have been together like that. Well, I know you, Caitlin, and that's a lot for a girl like you to handle."

"But I thought I'd forgiven both of them."

"I'm sure you did forgive them. But it's different now that you and Josh are going to get married. I heard a certain friend of mine explain that when we get married, we take every person we've ever slept with into the marriage bed with us."

"Eeeuuw."

"I don't mean literally. But it's like they're in our heads, and consequently they wind up in our beds."

Suddenly I remember something. "Hey, I'm the one who said that."

"Yeah, you were talking to Chloe, Allie, and Laura."

"And I wasn't thinking about the fact that my some-day husband might drag an old girlfriend into our bed." This thought makes me feel sick.

"It works both ways."

"I wonder how we get rid of them."

"I don't know. I know you were trying to get the girls to understand why abstinence is important. But I remember feeling worried that if I ever met that perfect guy and got married, well, I'd probably still have the old thing with Zach to deal with."

"But God forgave you. You moved on. Shouldn't that be the end of it?"

"Shouldn't it?" she echoes. "But that's not the case with you, is it? And crud, you didn't even sleep with any-one. It's like you're just an innocent bystander. That must feel like a stinking load of crud."

This almost makes me laugh. "You said it."

"Knowing you, I'm sure God will show you a way out, and then you can share this happy news with the rest of us."

"What if there is _no_ way out? What if I have to just accept what's happened and move on?"

"Then you do it and move on."

"But what if I can't?"

Now there's a long pause, and I'm afraid I've stumped her. "I guess it's better that you ask this question now than on your wedding night."

Gulp. "Yeah, I guess so."

"Hey, I'm sorry I'm not more help."

"No, you were."

"And I feel kind of bad being so up in the clouds while you're feeling so bad right now."

"Isn't that the way it goes? One of us is up; the other is down. It's like we take turns."

"Sometimes we're both up," she says, taking the positive route.

"Thank God, we're hardly ever down at the same time."

"That would be bad."

"If I don't talk to you before New York, knock 'em dead, okay?"

"I'll do my best, Caitlin."

"I'm praying for you."

"Back at you."

And then we hang up, and I don't think I'm any further along than I was before. But at least I don't feel like screaming now. I consider what Beanie said about God showing me the way out of this mess. And so, once again, I ask Him for help. And then just as simple as can be, I remember the Bible verse about going to a brother or sister if you have a problem and just telling them. Well, I guess I should've known that. But for some reason I resist. Maybe I just hope it will all go away on its own, like a bad rash or a fever.

DEAR GOD, HELP ME TO KNOW WHAT TO SAY TO
BOTH JENNY AND JOSH—AND WHEN TO SAY IT. I
KNOW THAT IT'S NOT REALLY THEIR FAULTS THAT
I'M FEELING SO MISERABLE RIGHT NOW. THEY'VE
CLEANED THEIR SLATES WITH YOU. BUT I BELIEVE
THAT THEY HAVE THE RIGHT TO KNOW THAT THIS
IS HURTING ME. PLEASE, HELP ME NOT TO BLOW
THIS WITH EITHER OF THEM. MORE THAN
ANYTHING, I'D LIKE TO BELIEVE THAT YOU HAVE A
DIVINE PURPOSE IN ALL THIS. I'M SURE YOU'RE NOT
PUTTING ME THROUGH THIS WRINGER OF PAIN FOR
NO REASON. THANK YOU. AMEN.

Friday, December 9

In Philippians 4:7 we're promised that God's peace (which
our minds can't fully understand) will keep our hearts
and minds safe in Jesus. And that's just how my week
has gone. And if I do say so myself, it's been nothing short
of miraculous. Of course, the verse before this one tells
us to pray and give thanks for everything. (And I've been
doing that too.)

So it feels as if I've skated through this week on
wheels of grace. Then finals week ended and I knew it
was time to lay my cards on the table with Jenny and
Josh. And since Josh is the man I love and am engaged to
marry, I decided it best to speak to him first.

Jenny had a test on Friday, so I was relieved that
Josh planned to pick me up yesterday after my last final.

There was no worry that she'd try to hitch a ride home with us. As selfish as that sounds, I couldn't have handled it.

Well, Josh picks me up around four and we haven't even left the campus before I tell him we need to talk. Those are my exact words. "We need to talk."

"Oh, man," he says. "I don't like the sound of that. Should I pull over and brace myself for something terrible?"

"Oh, I don't think—"

"Seriously, Caitlin, if you're going to tell me that God told you to break things off with me, or that you've fallen for another guy, I should pull over. I don't want to get us into a wreck."

I reach over and put my hand on his shoulder. "No, it's not like that. I still love you, Josh. I still want to marry you." But even as I say the latter, I'm not 100 percent sure. "It's just that I've had some things come up."

"Really, I can pull over before we get on the freeway."

"No, don't pull over, Josh. I think this might be easier for me to say if you're driving. I mean, I feel kind of silly about this, but I can't deny that I feel what I do. So just keep your eyes on the road and listen. And don't laugh."

"Hey, when my girl is this serious about something, I don't laugh."

"Good." So I remind him of the conversation that he and Jenny and I had on our last trip to campus.

"Yeah, I remember. It did feel a little awkward for a

minute or two. I was glad someone changed the subject.
Seems like it was you."

"It was." I try to remember just how I wanted to say
this. I thought I had a plan, but it seems to have evapo-
rated. "And in light of all the troubles in this world, like
wars and starvation and AIDS, well, I feel kind of silly for
being so disturbed by what probably seems like a very
minor thing to most people."

"Come on, Caitlin, spit it out."

I take in a deep breath. "Okay, here goes. Josh, it's
really been bugging me that you and Jenny had sex. I
know it was a long time ago, and I honestly thought I'd
forgotten all about it, or maybe just buried it, but suddenly it's all I can think about. It's like I wake up every
morning and get slapped in the face by the cold, hard
fact that my roommate has slept with my fiancé. It's
like I'm living out some stupid soap opera, and I don't even
watch soap operas."

Now I am starting to cry. "It's not that I don't love you.
I do, Josh. And I know that I forgave you a long time ago.
But it just feels like I'm being haunted by these memories. And then Beanie reminded me about how we'll take
anyone we've ever slept with into the marriage bed with
us—" But it's too late. I'm blubbering now and fishing
through my purse in search of a tissue.

Josh pulls over and he's just sitting there behind the
wheel like I just slugged him in the stomach. I can tell
he's totally stunned.

"I told you it was stupid, Josh. I told you I—"

"No," he says in a strong voice. "It's not stupid."

Then he turns and looks at me, and his face looks pale and serious, like he's hurting nearly as much as I am. And this makes me feel absolutely horrible. I mean, what kind of girl would do this to someone like Josh Miller? Josh, who has spent the last four years devoting his life to following God, who took heavy class loads to finish Bible college with honors, and who is now employed as an underpaid and overworked youth pastor whose concern for starving children in Mexico keeps him awake at night trying to think of new ways to raise money. What kind of horrible monster am I? Maybe God should just reach down and smack me right now.

"Oh, Josh," I say, reaching for him. "I'm so sorry."

But he shakes his head and gently pushes me back.

"I never should've mentioned—"

"No, Caitlin, listen to me, okay?"

I nod and sit back in my seat. I'm sure that he must hate me now. He's probably about to tell me that this is all just an unfortunate mistake, that we should simply part and quietly go our separate ways, and that he's been through this kind of thing with me one time too many. I mean, seriously. Why am I always hurting this guy? What is wrong with me? But at least I manage to keep my mouth closed. I just wish he would say something. Anything.

"You are absolutely right to feel this way," he begins. "I don't even know why I never considered this before." He pushes a stray piece of blond hair off of his forehead and sighs. "I guess it was so far back, so long ago... I think I sort of forgot about it too."

"Until I brought it all back."

"But that's not your fault, Caitlin." He reaches for my hand now. "You can't pretend not to feel what you really feel. And I should've known that this was something we'd need to talk about. I guess because I made my peace with God, well, I probably hoped that just finished it."

"And shouldn't it?" I look into his eyes. "I mean, God doesn't throw old sins back in our faces. Once He forgives us, that's it." I look away now. "It's my fault for dredging this stuff up. I shouldn't—"

"I don't think you dredged anything up. I think that God is just giving us an opportunity to clear this up between us. And as hard as it is to hear this and to be reminded of what a selfish jerk I was back then, I think it's good."

He takes both my hands. "And I swear to you, Caitlin, I am so sorry that I had sex with Jenny. I wish more than anything in this world that I could give myself to you as a virgin. And—and it means so much to me that you've saved yourself for—" Now he starts to cry. And suddenly we're both sobbing and clinging to each other and I'm thinking how could I possibly have had bad thoughts about this man? How could I possibly love him any more than I do right now?

"Oh, Josh," I say through my tears. "I love you more than anyone on earth. And I know that I need to totally forgive you for what happened with Jenny. And with

God's help that's exactly what I'm going to do."

"Do you really mean that?"

I nod. Then we hug for a while longer. Finally we pull apart, and I take in a deep breath. "Guess it's a good thing you pulled over," I say. And we both laugh.

Later on that night, we go for coffee and discuss this whole thing some more. Not that I want to so much. I actually feel like my issues with Josh were beginning to get resolved right there on the highway. And I have no doubt that God had a hand in that. But I think Josh needs to say a few more things. And I'll admit that I was glad to hear them.

"I want you to know that Jenny was the only girl I've ever had sex with," he admits. "I know that there were rumors going around school that I'd done it with other girls, but those rumors weren't true. I'm embarrassed to say that I did nothing to stop the rumors either. I thought it was cool that kids just assumed I was doing that."

"Yeah, I understand how that worked."

"And tell me if you don't want to hear this, but I hope that you will. What happened between me and Jenny..." He pauses, as if to gauge my interest, and I simply nod and attempt to act like I'm not glomming on to his every word. "Well, it was pretty awful and awkward for both of us. Believe me, it was nothing like you see in the movies. And I was actually so embarrassed that after that I never wanted to talk to her again. I think that's one of the reasons I started hanging around you so much then."

He kind of laughs. "And I knew that you didn't even want me around. But it's like you were such a comfort to me." Then he reaches over and takes my hand. "And of course, I was falling in love."

"You were falling in love way back then?"

"Oh, you knew I was. You knew that you were running the show too. I would've done anything for you."

I smile. "Guess it's a good thing I made that commitment to God. Who knows what might've happened otherwise?"

"Yeah, we'd probably be living in a trailer with five or six kids by now."

And even though we laughed pretty hard over that image, I knew that it probably wasn't that far from the truth. Because I'd had it bad for Josh way back then too. Thank God for calling me to something far better.

DEAR GOD, ONCE AGAIN, ALL I CAN SAY IS THANK YOU! YOU ARE SO AMAZING AND WONDERFUL. THE WAY YOU CAN TAKE OUR CRUD AND CHANGE IT INTO SOMETHING BEAUTIFUL JUST BLOWS MY MIND. THANKS FOR JOSH AND HOW MUCH I LOVE HIM. PLEASE HELP ME TO PUT AWAY THIS BURDEN, AND HELP ME TO KNOW WHEN (OR EVEN IF) I SHOULD TALK TO JENNY. AMEN.

ELEVEN

Thursday, December 15

God must've known how badly college students needed Christmas break. Okay, so the university calls it winter break. Whatever. But I am so glad to be back in my hometown, so glad that my grandma let me house-sit, and so glad that I get to sleep in. Life is exceedingly good.

I decided to give Jenny a chance to relax after finals week, before I call and invite her to come visit me at my grandma's house. "Do you remember where it is?"

"Do I remember?" she says with excitement. "We had some great times there the last time we house-sat for her. Is Beanie coming too?"

So I fill her in on Beanie's New York trip. "She just called me this morning. She still doesn't know if she's been accepted for sure, but she said it's looking good. She should be home by Saturday."

Then Jenny comes over, and I ask her how her weight-gain plan is coming. "I feel sort of bad that we're not doing our nightly weigh-ins."

"Yeah, me too. And I'll admit that my mom made a comment that almost got me going. But you know what I did?"

"I have no idea."

"I told myself that if I gave in, it would be like she was controlling me again. You know what I mean? Like just because she makes some lame comment about food or weight, doesn't mean that I have to go all anorexic again."

"Wow, that's real progress, Jenny."

She nods. "My counselor says that it's all about control and empowerment. I need to know that I have control in my life, but not through things like losing another pound."

We talk some more, and I'm surprised at how naturally our conversation just evolves into what's been bothering me. And it's a relief because I wasn't really sure that I would bring it up.

"That's kind of like something I've been going through," I tell her. "It started a couple of weeks ago, and I got so bummed that I kind of quit talking to you."

"So it wasn't just finals."

"No, it wasn't."

"Well, that's good because I was starting to think you were kind of freaky, you know? Totally obsessed with finals."

"No, I was totally obsessed with something else."

"What?" She leans forward with concern.

"I hadn't thought about it in years. In fact, I'd actually forgotten about it. But then on that night when Josh brought us back to school, you know when we were reminiscing about the good old days?"

She nodded with a troubled brow. "Yeah?"

"Well, it suddenly occurred to me that my roommate had slept with my fiancé." I kind of make a face. "I know it sounds like something straight out of 'All My Children.' But seriously, it kind of freaked me out."

Jenny almost looked like she was about to cry.

"I'm not saying this to make you feel bad," I say quickly. "I guess it's more of a confession. It's like the more I thought about it, the madder I got at you. And I know that's totally unfair. It was just making me miserable."

"I can understand that, Cate."

"But I prayed for God to get me through finals, and then I talked to Josh about it and—"

"What did he say?" She was sitting up straight now, kind of like she felt indignant.

"Only that he was really sorry about it. He feels bad that it happened, and he's even mentioned that after I clear the air with you, he plans to make an official apology to you."

"To me?"

"Yeah. He knows that God has forgiven him. And that

I have too. But he still feels badly for you. He knows that you got hurt as well."

Now Jenny is crying, and I can't help but cry too. I move over to the couch where she's sitting and put my arm around her. "Jenny, I'm sorry to make you feel bad. It really wasn't my motive. I just wanted things to get better between us. You're a good friend, and I really love you. But it's like there was this wall growing between us. I couldn't stand it."

She sniffs and nods. "I know. I could feel it too. And to be honest, I've wondered about that in the past. I mean, it is kind of weird that we became friends. And for a long time Josh was so out of the picture that I almost forgot the history we had. Then suddenly we're rooming together, and then Josh is proposing to you and—"

Now she just bursts into full-blown tears. She is sobbing so hard that I think she must be in pain. And I don't know what to do. I'm actually considering calling someone. Like maybe Aunt Steph could help out. So I pray that God will show me what to do and that somehow He will comfort her. I reach for the box of tissues that Grandma always keeps nearby, and I place them in front of her. And finally she stops.

"Wow," she says as she blows her nose on a tissue. "I don't know where that came from."

I just shake my head. "Me neither. But I'm sorry if it came from me."

She sighs and looks down at the crumpled tissues in her lap. "No, it's not from you. Not exactly. But maybe this thing with you and Josh helped to flip my memory switch."

"How's that?"

And then she starts telling me about this guy she met at the start of her junior year at college. She had still been going to the Christian college where she and Beanie and Anna had gone right out of high school. Ironically, she was the only one of the three who stuck with it that long. "And I would be there now," she tells me, "if it weren't for Peter."

"I never heard about this guy."

"No one has. And there's a reason. Peter and I hit it off from the start. The problem was Peter had a girl-friend."

"Oh."

She nods. "But Peter and this girl had been going together since high school, and I think he was getting a little bored with their relationship. Anyway, he and I would just meet for coffee or walk to class together. No big deal. We mostly liked to talk. And I suppose in all hon-esty we were flirting a little too. But it's not like he was married. And I guess I felt myself getting more and more attracted to him. I think he saw me as something a little more risky and exciting than Meredith. No offense, but Meredith kind of reminded me of you when it came to things like abstinence and being so devout. I really didn't like her much."

"Thanks a lot."

"Okay, that's where the comparison stops. Meredith

was like a stick in the mud about everything. She even thought that playing cards was sinful. But you're not like that. You're fun and smart and you're not judgmental."

"Okay, I feel a little better."

"Come on, Cate, this is my story."

"Sorry."

"So by spring term, Peter and I were seeing quite a lot of each other. And it was actually starting to get fairly romantic. Before long we were sneaking around to be together. He kept saying that he would break up with Meredith, but it was like she had some kind of hold on him. Even so, I really thought that eventually he was going to get sick of her. I mean, everyone else was."

Now Jenny looks almost as if she's going to cry again. "And then I did something really stupid. It's like I was back in high school again, like I'd never learned my lesson the first time. I mean, I knew Peter wanted it too. In fact, he wanted it way more than I did. And he kept hinting. He'd even call me up and read verses out of Song of Solomon. And you know how passionate that book can get."

I nod. I am thinking this guy is a total jerk, but I don't say this.

"And so I finally gave in. I actually thought that if I slept with him, it would cinch the deal. He'd leave Meredith, and we'd get married and live happily ever after."

I'm feeling kind of sick now. Bad for Jenny as well as these other two. And I'm wondering why we humans make such stupid decisions sometimes. But I'm trying to keep my expression even. I don't want Jenny to know how much it hurts to hear this.

"We did it a few times, and believe me, Cate, it was NOT that great. Maybe it was because it was his first time and only my second. But I'll tell you this now—it was not worth it. Still, it's like I was driven at the time. Like I was going to win this man or die trying. And then suddenly it was over. Peter cut me off like a bad habit." She kind of smiles. "I guess I was."

"What happened then?"

"Well, I was devastated, of course. I tried to call him or accidentally run into him, but he was either gone or surrounded by his buddies. I learned later that he'd gone to their church back home, where Meredith's dad was the pastor, and he'd confessed his sin with me, repented, and asked for help."

"Oh."

"And by the end of the school year, I learned that Peter and Meredith had gotten engaged, and that the wedding was set for August."

"August."

"Yeah, about the same time I started going anorexic again. Pathetic, isn't it?"

"No, it's just sad."

"Actually, my counselor tells me it's textbook."

"Oh."

"That's how it is with some of us, Cate. We gotta learn everything the hard way."

"Well, don't take this wrong, but I think Peter sounds like a complete jerk and you are so much better off without him."

"I know that now. But it hurt back then. In fact, it still hurts now. Oh, not about Peter so much, more about the way I let myself, and subsequently God, down."

"And that's why you transferred to the university?"

"That and to be with you. Somehow I knew my old friend Cate could help me through this. And see, you have. I'm just sorry that I had to be the source of so much pain for you these past couple of weeks. I wish you would've said something."

"I didn't know what to say."

"Yeah, it's kind of awkward. But if it's any consolation, I can barely remember what happened with Josh that one time. We'd both been drinking, and I was hoping I could get him to dump you and take me to the prom." She rolls her eyes. "How's that for a true confession. I can't believe you can even stand me."

"That was a long time ago, Jenny."

"But I'm still pretty flaky. I mean, look at the thing with Peter."

"But he had a lot to do with that too. He strung you along. And trust me, he's probably paying for it now." I consider the marriage bed metaphor and just shake my head. "And Meredith too. It can't be too great being married to someone like that."

We talk for so long that Jenny ends up spending the night. "Like old times," she says as we make microwave popcorn and tune in to the classic movie station.

And once again, I can see how it is important to bring these old issues to the surface. It not only allowed Jenny and me to clear some things up, but it gave her a chance to tell me a story that had been festering inside of her. And maybe these wounds will begin to heal for her now. I just hope she learned a lesson through all this. And I'm sure she has.

And suddenly I'm thinking that Liz and Jenny need to get better acquainted. I mean, Liz has just assumed that Jenny is some Miss Perfect, church-going, Goody Two-shoes...and the truth is, Jenny's made some of the exact same mistakes as Liz. Maybe I'll tell Jenny a little more about Liz and see if she wants to join us for coffee next time.

DEAR GOD, YOU ARE MYSTERIOUS AND MARVELOUS. YOU TIPTOE AROUND IN OUR LIVES AND MAKE MIRACLES BLOSSOM FROM DUMPSTERS. YOU TAKE OUR SORROW AND GRIEF AND WEAVE IT INTO A CLOAK OF GLADNESS AND JOY. YOU ARE THE GREAT REDEEMER AND YOU DELIGHT IN DELIVERING YOUR CHILDREN. MIGHTY GOD, I LOVE YOU! AMEN.

TWELVE

Monday, December 19

I've never seen **Beanie** so ecstatically
happy. It's like she's literally glowing. If I didn't know better, I'd assume she was in love. And in a way I guess she
is. But she's in love with Pratt, her new design school
that's just offered her a full scholarship. She told Jenny
and me the details today. We'd met at the mall to do a
little last-minute Christmas shopping.

"I can't believe this is happening to me," she said
after we met at the food court. "It's like a dream." We
ordered our food from separate places, then I found the
last available table, clear on the other side and still
sticky from the last occupants. I wiped it down with a
napkin and waited for my friends to join me.

"Okay, spill the beans, Beanie," I said once we were
all seated.

She laughed. "Haven't heard that one in a while."

Then she sat up straighter and, in an I-have-arrived voice, said, "I go by Sabrina Jacobs now."

"Such a sophisticated name." I nodded my approval.

"Such a sophisticated girl," added Jenny. "Just look at her. She looks like she stepped off the cover of 'Vogue.'"

And Jenny was right. It's as if Beanie had really come into her own lately. I mean, she wasn't only dressed fantastically with tall brown boots and a chocolate brown wool suit to die for, but she looked absolutely stunning too. I know she's lost weight, but I wouldn't dare mention this in front of Jenny.

Not that Beanie was skinny; she's not. But with her height and dark good looks, well, she just looks very hot. And I noticed guys looking our way today. I have a feeling it was Beanie who was catching their eye this time. A fun change since high school when we always felt it was Jenny's Catherine Zeta-Jones kind of good looks that got all the male attention. But back to Beanie.

"It's a full scholarship," Beanie told us. "And it's one of the best design schools in the country. I'll finish up their undergraduate program by summer, since my credits were mostly transferable, and I'll start the graduate program next fall. I get to intern with one of the big designers, and my counselor told me that based on my portfolio, it will be someone big!" The pitch of her voice had gotten higher, and for a moment I expected her to let out a squeal, but she was trying to keep up her sophisticated persona.

"Oh, Beanie!" I exclaimed. "I am so excited for you. That must be so cool. I can't even imagine going to school in New York City. Manhattan even."

"Well, most of my classes are in Brooklyn. But hey, New York is New York. And even though I was only there a few days, I felt totally at home. When I told my mom this—do you know what she said?"

"What?" asked Jenny.

"She said that's probably because that's where my dad was from."

"Wow. Amazing."

"Have you seen your dad?" asked Jenny.

Beanie shook her head. "Someday, when I have time or when I'm rich and famous, I think I'll hire someone to see if they can locate him through one of those Internet searches." Then she shrugged. "Or not. I guess if he doesn't care about seeing me, then maybe I don't care either."

"More about New York," I said, eager to change the subject.

"When I went for my first interview, I about fell over to see all the big designers lined up right next to the school. There was Liz Claiborne, Gitano, Benetton, Perry Ellis..just to name a few. I was so impressed."

"I am so envious," said Jenny. "Your life is so exciting, Beanie."

"Beanie has been working hard," I reminded Jenny. "She has real talent, and it's about time she got some recognition and a good break."

Jenny nodded. "I know. And I'm so happy for her. I just wish I could go with her. Be a mouse in her pocket, you know?"

Beanie held open her jacket pocket. "Hop in, little Jenny Mouse. Come on along." Then she laughed. "The truth is you'd have to be the size of a mouse to fit into my room with me. While I was there I met the girls I'll be rooming with, and the room is about ten foot square—for four girls. Can you imagine? They said the real bugaboo is closet space. Some girls have to rent storage spaces to hold their off-season clothes."

"What will you do?" asked Jenny.

"I'm thinking I'll go minimalist," said Beanie. "But it'll be a challenge, since you have to look like a million bucks while you're interning if you want to be taken seriously." She sighed. "I have to admit that some of this kind of bugs me. I mean, I love design. No doubt about that. But it's the creative part that I get into. I'm not sure how I really feel about the money end of the industry."

"Kind of hard to separate that," commented Jenny.

"Yeah, but I'm praying for God to lead me in this."

"He will," I assured her. "Just keep your eyes on Him."

"That may be a challenge," said Jenny. And we both looked at her as if we expected more. "Well, you know. The fashion industry is probably one of the most shallow, worldly industries out there."

Beanie nodded. "I realize that. But I still have to wonder why things can't change. Why can't a godly woman design clothing that honors God and looks attractive on women?"

Jenny held up her drink cup as if to toast her. "Why not?"

I held up my cup too. "Why not?"

And Beanie joined us. "Here's to why not."

We finished our lunch and visit, then all went our separate ways to shop. We decided it would be easier this way, since the mall was crowded and we all had different places to go. "But I want you two to come over for dinner this week," I told them. "I thought you might help me do a little wedding planning." So we agreed on Friday and then set off to brace ourselves against the crowds and the tinny-sounding Christmas music playing everywhere.

But I'll have to admit, I kind of enjoyed the whole Christmas-at-the-mall scene today—distracted shoppers rushing around overloaded with bags, fidgety kids waiting in line to see Santa, and all the cheesy mall decorations they bring out of mothballs every year, shortly after Halloween. Well, I thought it was all rather charming. Maybe it's because I'm in love and engaged and just slightly giddy. Maybe I'm seeing the world through rose-colored glasses. But hey, I actually liked it.

As usual, I didn't have a whole lot of money to spend on gifts, but after several hours, I think I finally got them nailed. Of course, Josh was the hardest. What do you get your fiancé on the first Christmas that you're officially together? I know that neither of us have much money, so I'm sure not expecting anything fancy or expensive. But I wanted to get him something nice, something that he would have years from now to remember.

And okay, it probably sounds a little old-fashioned, but I decided to get him cuff links—the kind they engrave initials onto. But instead of getting JM (Josh Miller), I decided to get JC (Josh and Caitlin). And after the lady showed me the finished product, it occurred to me that JC also stands for Jesus Christ. I thought that was pretty cool.

While I was waiting for the cuff links, I even looked at guys' wedding rings, since I realized that this is something I'm supposed to eventually get for Josh. And I found several in platinum that I think would look nice on him. I decided that when I get the ring, I'll have it engraved too. I think I'll have it engraved to say "JC Forever," and maybe I could get that on my wedding band too.

Then I searched and searched until I found the perfect romantic card. And okay, cuff links and a card isn't much of a gift, but it's the best I can do right now. I have a feeling Josh will appreciate it, and I'm hoping he'll wear the cuff links at our wedding. Yeah, yeah, call me corny or sentimental or whatever. But that's just me.

Wednesday, December 21
"I just got a call from Saint Matthew's," Josh told me on the phone this morning. "There's been a cancellation on June 1."

"Really?" I asked.

"The only problem is that it's the evening slot. What do you think about an evening wedding?"

I considered this. "I guess I never thought about it. I don't know why."

"Well, do you want to go over to the church and check it out with me? Have you ever been inside it before?"

"No, but I've admired the architecture from the outside."

"Are you busy for lunch today?"

"Hmm, let me check my calendar," I teased.

"Can you squeeze me in?"

"I always have time for you, Josh."

So after a quick lunch, we went over to Saint Matthew's. The secretary recognized Josh right off.

"It's little Joshua Miller," she said in a sugary voice. "Do you remember me from second grade Sunday school?"

He smiled and shook her hand. "I sure do. And this is my fiancée Caitlin O'Conner. Caitlin, this is Mrs. Price."

"A pleasure to meet you, dear. Goodness, you two make a very lovely couple. I can imagine it's going to be a beautiful wedding. Are you overwhelmed with all the planning, dear?"

I smiled at her. "I'm trying not to be."

She nodded. "Good for you. It is only one day, you know. What really counts is what comes afterward." She winked at Josh. "Mr. Price and I just celebrated our fortieth wedding anniversary."

We both congratulated her, then Josh assured her that he still knew his way around the church, if she had more important matters to take care of. To our relief, she does. Then Josh took my hand, as if I were a princess, and slowly walked me into the sanctuary, which I must admit is quite beautiful.

It's not the kind of velvet-drape beautiful where things are carved and gold plated and over the top. It's more a stately elegance of old wooden surfaces that have been worn and polished over many years until there's a warm patina that just glows. And I was relieved to see that the carpet wasn't red. For some reason I have a problem with walking down a red-carpeted aisle. I guess I don't want to feel as if I'm at the Academy Awards and about to get my first Oscar. But this carpet is a nice dark mossy shade that goes well with the wood.

And then there are the stained glass windows. All those jewel-toned colors radiating light almost take your breath away. But suddenly I remembered something.

"Oh, Josh, the windows are magnificent. But if it's nighttime, they'll be dark and it won't be as pretty."

He considered this. "But it will only be seven o'clock. And it will be June. We'll have daylight for at least two more hours."

I smiled and hugged him. "You're so smart."

He laughed. "I hope you'll always be so easy to impress."

Then we both stand there for several minutes, just allowing the quiet ambience to surround us. And it sounds weird, because I really don't ever think of God as being confined to one place, but I was sure I felt His presence in this room. And I know Josh felt it too. It was almost like a hallowed moment. Neither of us said anything but simply turned and left.

"It's perfect," I told him once we were in the hallway.

Josh smiled. "I'm glad you like it. I actually have a lot of good childhood memories in this church."

"But what about the reception?"

"There's a room that they use," he told me. "Do you want to see it?"

"Of course." And feeling as if we've hit the jackpot, I couldn't help but smile as he led me down a hallway then finally opened a set of double doors. But this room wasn't anything like I'd hoped. Besides the fact that the ceiling felt low and the carpeting was dark blue, there were no windows, and it felt claustrophobic.

"Not so great, is it?" said Josh.

"It doesn't feel right to me."

"Me neither. Well, we can't figure it all out in a day, Catie."

"That's right. And I have no doubts that God knows the perfect place for a reception."

As Josh drove me back to my grandma's house, it began to snow. "Oh, look," I said. "Do you think we'll have a white Christmas after all?"

He frowned. "Not according to the weather guy on Channel 9 news."

"I hope he's wrong."

"So where do you think would be the perfect place for a reception?" he asked as he stopped at a red light.

I paused to consider this. "I'm not sure. But since it'll be June, it might be nice to be outside, or does that seem weird?"

"Not to me. I think an outdoor reception would be awesome."

"But I don't really want to have it in someone's backyard. And I don't think any of the parks around here would work. Well, unless..."

"Unless what, Catie?"

"Well, I don't think it'd really work."

"What?"

"Remember the spot by the lake where you proposed?"

Josh smiled as the light turned green. "I'll never forget that night."

"Wouldn't it be amazing to have a reception by the lake?"

He nodded. "But that spot is kind of tricky. There isn't any parking, and people would have to walk a ways in."

"And that'd be hard bringing in things like the cake and chairs and stuff." I felt slightly disappointed. "But if I could wave my magic wand and get everyone there and everything in place, I know it would be beautiful."

Then we're at my grandma's house and it looked to me as if the Channel 9 weatherman was wrong because the snow was coming down hard and heavy. "Isn't it beautiful?" I said as he pulled into the driveway.

"Yes." He leaned over and kissed me on the cheek. "You are."

Of course, this made me laugh. "Thanks for lunch, Josh."

"Glad you don't turn your nose up at fast food."

"Hey, any food with you is a feast."

This cracked him up. "We're turning into a couple of cornballs."

"Cornballs." I laughed. "That's a good one."

Then we kissed and I let him go so he could make it back to work before his lunch hour ended.

DEAR GOD, THANKS FOR GIVING US THE PERFECT PLACE TO SAY OUR WEDDING VOWS. I KNOW THAT OUR PROMISES TO LOVE, HONOR, AND CHERISH WOULD BE VALID NO MATTER WHERE WE SAY IT— EVEN IF IT WAS IN THE MIDDLE OF A BUSY INTERSECTION ON MAIN STREET. BUT I AM SO THANKFUL THAT YOU LOVE US ENOUGH TO GIVE US A BEAUTIFUL SANCTUARY LIKE SAINT MATTHEW'S. AND THANK YOU FOR BEING THERE WITH US TODAY. I LOVE YOU! AMEN.

THIRTEEN

Thursday, December 22

It's about nine in the morning when Josh
calls me with an urgent sound to his voice. "Caitlin, I think
I know where we can have the reception."

"Really? Where?"

"Are you busy right now?"

"No, but can you get off work in the middle of the
morning?"

He laughs. "You'll have to figure out that a pastor's
workweek isn't exactly a nine-to-five gig. Between
Sundays and evening services, Bible studies, youth group
meetings—"

"Okay, I get it. When will you be here?"

"Ten minutes."

But Josh won't tell me where we're going as he drives
across town. For a moment I think it's the same place
that he proposed, but then he drives past the park and

keeps going on around the lake. And since everything has turned into a winter wonderland, I don't even care where he's headed. I'm just staring out the window in amazement, drinking in the loveliness. The sun has just come out, and the lake looks amazing surrounded by white snow.

"Do you know where we're going?" he finally asks.

"No, should I?"

"You've been there before."

"Really? With you?"

"Unfortunately."

"Unfortunately?" I turn and look curiously at him. "What do you mean?"

Then he explains how he brought me up here during his senior year in high school. "It was my cousin's birthday party. And I acted like a total moron that night."

"Oh, yeah," I say. "I do remember. You got drunk."

He nods. "I can't even remember the details. Except that you were enraged and I was a jerk. Did I ever tell you I was sorry?"

I laugh. "Several times. As I recall, you showed up with roses and all kinds of things. But by then I was ready to dump you anyway."

Josh laughs. "We've been through a lot, Catie."

"So we're going to your cousin's house?" I still feel a little confused by this.

"Actually, Tom doesn't live there. I should probably explain. Tom graduated the same year as I did, but then he went into the air force straight out of high school. It was all he'd ever dreamed of since he was a little kid. Of course, my aunt and uncle were really disappointed since they would've gladly sent him anywhere to go to school. But Tom wanted the excitement."

I can tell by the sad tone of Josh's voice that this isn't a happy story. "What happened?"

"Tom was in a helicopter that was shot down in Iraq last year."

"Oh, I'm so sorry."

He sighs deeply. "Me too."

"Are you sure we should go see his parents?"

"Yes, I talked to Aunt Patty this morning, and she said they'd love to have us come out. They are so excited to meet you."

"Did you ask about the reception?"

"No. I thought we'd just see how it goes."

"I don't know, Josh. This all seems kind of sad to me. I feel so bad about your cousin. I remember that night and how much I resented him for encouraging you to drink like that. This just feels weird."

"I know. I was afraid that might be your reaction, so you have to let me tell you the rest of the story."

"The rest of the story?"

"When the war in Iraq began, I started feeling worried about Tom, and I began e-mailing him on a regular basis. At first he brushed off any talk about God. But then something happened—something that really shook him up—and suddenly he was interested. He gave his life to God over there. I couldn't believe it at first. But then I discovered it wasn't that unusual. Apparently lots of people in the service find God in the midst of war."

"Wow. I guess that just shows how God can bring good out of anything."

"Of course, this wasn't much consolation to Uncle Bob and Aunt Patty since they're not believers. But I think they did appreciate that Tom and I stayed in touch while he was over there."

Now Josh is pulling up a long tree-lined driveway, and I'm trying to remember what it looked like when Josh brought me here back in high school. As I recall, there were cars parked everywhere, and of course, it wasn't all snowy and white like this. But really, it feels like it was a totally different place. I don't even recall that it was on a lake. But then it was nighttime, it was raining, and I don't recall going out back.

"Good thing I've got it in four-wheel drive." He steps on the gas and easily takes us up the small incline. Then he parks in front of the house, gets out, and runs around to the other side to open my door. I am feeling nervous about meeting Josh's relatives. It's obvious they are wealthy, but more than that, I'm still feeling bad about their son. It's like I'm grieving. But how would this make sense to anyone?

"There you are," says a woman with white hair that's stylishly cut to turn under at her shoulders. Despite the color of her hair, her face seems young, though I detect sadness in her eyes. "And this must be the remarkable Caitlin." She gives me a hug. "I'm Aunt Patty, but you can call me Patty." Then she steps back to really look at me. "You're just as pretty as they say. Here, let me take your coats."

As we give her our coats, I compliment her on the beautiful home. And it really is beautiful. Nothing like I remember from that night when the lights were turned low and there were about a hundred rowdy kids in various stages of intoxication packing it like sardines. This was like something altogether different.

"Bob is on the phone. Why don't you come into the family room and sit down." Patty leads us through the spacious foyer and through an elegant but not overly decorated living room, where a grand piano dominates a corner by a window. "I have to apologize for our lack of Christmas decorations this year," she says sadly. "I know I must seem like a Scrooge, but I just didn't have the heart for it."

"I can understand," I tell her. "Josh told me about Tom, and I am so sorry. I only met him once, but I can't even imagine how you must be feeling."

She pauses at the edge of the living room to turn and look into my eyes. "You're right. It is one of those things that no one can imagine. Not unless you go through it yourself, and I certainly hope you never do. Tom was our only child, and I miss him every day."

"I miss him too," says Josh. And I can tell by his voice that he's choking up. "I still can't believe he's gone."

Then she reaches out and gives Josh a big hug. "You remind me of him, Josh. Oh, I know you boys were different, but there's something of the Miller family in both of you that I can't quite put my finger on."

Then she takes us into another area that opens up into a huge family room, which connects to a large kitchen. And both these rooms have floor-to-ceiling windows that look out onto the lake.

I think I actually gasp when I see it. "Oh, this is so beautiful."

She seems surprised by my reaction, but then she turns and follows my gaze out the windows and nods. "Yes, it's quite pretty with the snow." She glances over at the tall rock fireplace. "I guess I should've asked Bob to light a fire for us."

"How about if I do that?" suggests Josh.

Patty brightens. "Oh, would you?" Then she turns to me. "Caitlin, would you like a cup of tea?"

"I'd love one."

"How about something for you, Josh?" she calls as I follow her to the kitchen. "I'm sure you're not a tea drinker. I still have coffee that's fairly fresh."

"That sounds great," he calls as he wads up some newspaper.

And so we visit with Josh's aunt, and she talks some more about Tom and how hard this year has been for her and how Christmas will never be the same. And I feel so sad that I'm afraid I won't be able to keep it together. I ask her where the powder room is, and I go in there and cry.

I know it's silly and emotional, but I just can't help

myself. It's as if my heart is breaking for her, and I don't even know how she can hold on. Like there's no hope at all. Finally, I think I've got it under control. I splash some cold water on my face, dry my eyes, and return to where we were having our tea.

"There she is," says Patty as I emerge, I'm sure, with reddened eyes. "Bob finally got off the phone and wants to—" She stops in midsentence. "Oh, dear, have you been crying?"

Of course, this only makes me start losing it again. "I'm sorry."

She puts a hand on my shoulder and guides me to the sofa. "Whatever is wrong?"

"I'm just so sad for you—for your loss, I mean." Then I notice Josh's uncle sitting in a leather chair by the fireplace.

"Has Patty been depressing you with—?"

"No, no," I say quickly. "Josh just told me about it as we were driving up, and I felt so badly. Really, I'm sorry. I didn't mean to—"

"Caitlin has a very tender heart," Josh says as he comes and sits on the other side of me. "In fact, she's the one who got me so interested in helping out with the orphan mission in Mexico."

I turn and smile at Josh, thankful that he's changing the subject.

"Tell us more about that, Josh," says Patty.

So Josh launches into the story about how I fell apart the first time I saw the garbage-dump kids. He goes on to explain how this led to FAD, and how we plan to go down there after we're married.

"That's so amazing," says Patty. "You two kids are something. Imagine wanting to devote your life to helping underprivileged children."

I shrug. "I guess it's just a God-thing."

She seems to consider this. "Well, I suppose there are a lot of God-things I don't fully understand."

"You and me both," says Josh. Then he inquires about his uncle's investment business, which is apparently run from their home. And then his uncle invites him back to his office to see some new computer thing that he's still trying to get the bugs out of.

"You kids just seem to know more about electronics than us old fogies," his uncle says as they leave the room. "Tom was always the one I went to when I got stuck on my computer."

"We reserved a place for the wedding," I tell Patty as she pours us another cup of tea.

"Where?"

"Saint Matthew's."

She smiles. "Oh, lovely. That's where we go to church. Bob and I were married there too. Nearly thirty years ago."

"It's going to be an evening wedding," I tell her, glad that we've finally talking about something that won't make me cry. "At first I was worried that we'd miss out on the beautiful stained glass, but Josh reminded me that it'll be June then, and the sun will still be out at seven."

"A June wedding. How perfect. And where is the reception?"

Now I feel uncomfortable. No way can I mention that Josh was hoping these poor grieving people would allow us to use their beautiful lakeside home. "I don't know. We can't afford much, but I wasn't too impressed with the meeting room in the church. And even a hotel feels kind of impersonal to me. I'm not really sure what we'll do yet, but I know that God will provide someplace special."

Now Patty has this faraway look in her eye. "I used to dream of having a wedding reception out here. I could just imagine Tom and his bride down by the lake. Can you imagine how lovely the photos would be?"

I nod. "It would be amazing."

Then she looks as if she's had a revelation. "Oh, why don't you kids have the reception here?"

"Oh no. We couldn't impose on you like that. Especially not after all the grief you've been—"

"No, no." She's standing up now and pacing as if she's staging a play. "I can just imagine it. Oh, it would be so wonderful. We'd have lights and music and that deck down below would be a perfect dance floor."

She turns and looks at me now, and I can see hope in her eyes. "Oh, please, Caitlin. Wouldn't you consider having it here? It would give me something to think about besides, well, you know. It would give me something to work toward. And don't forget that Josh is very special to us. He and Tom literally grew up together. Please, tell me that you'll think about—"

"Think about what?" Bob says as the two guys come back into the room.

Patty rushes over to her husband and grabs him by the hand. "Oh, Bob, I've just had the most marvelous idea. Tell me that you'll agree."

He kind of smiles at this. "Why don't you tell me what it is first."

"I want Josh and Caitlin to have their wedding reception out here. I've always dreamed of having something like that. And who better to have it for than these two?"

Bob's brow creases as he considers this, but by the way he's slowly nodding, I can tell that he's intrigued. "I think it's a great idea. But what about them, Patty? Maybe they don't want to have it in a campy place like this. Maybe they've booked some huge ballroom with crystal chandeliers and marble floors, did you think about that?"

I laugh. "I don't go for that kind of thing."

"Me neither," says Josh. "Actually, we'd love to have an outdoor reception."

"See!" Patty points her finger in the air triumphantly. "Tell me you'll consider it, Josh. You don't have to decide today. But please just think about it."

"I don't have to think about it. I love the idea."

"What about you, Caitlin?" asks Bob. "You may need time to think about it. I don't want you to feel like Patty twisted your arm."

"I would love to have our reception here. I think this is the most beautiful home I've ever been in. And your view of the lake is spectacular. I couldn't imagine any place better. But I don't want to put you guys out. I know it would involve some work and—"

"Work is what I need right now," says Patty. "I need something I can plan for and plunge into, something that will take energy. I love to garden, but I know I'll need something to motivate me this year. You kids having your reception here would be the best thing anyone could do for me."

So it's settled. And even if their home wasn't the most gorgeous place I've seen, I would still want to have it with them. I understand what Patty is saying about needing something like that to help her to move on. But more than that, I just really fell in love with those two people, and I think that God is up to something bigger than a wedding reception in their lives. I know that I'll be praying for them from now on.

DEAR GOD, AS ALWAYS, YOU ARE AMAZINGLY AWESOME. AND YOU'VE DONE IT AGAIN. NOT ONLY IS THE LOCATION FOR OUR WEDDING RECEPTION THE GREATEST, BUT PATTY AND BOB FEEL LIKE LONG-LOST RELATIVES TO ME. AND I KNOW THAT YOU WANT TO MAKE THEM PART OF YOUR FAMILY TOO. PLEASE, SHOW THEM WHO YOU REALLY ARE AND GIVE THEM THE KIND OF ETERNAL HOPE THAT IS SO ABSENT FROM THEIR LIVES. AMEN.

FOURTEEN

Friday, December 23

Beanie and Jenny came to dinner tonight. I figured it was a good excuse for me to work on my culinary skills. Unfortunately for them, my culinary skills really need some work. But they didn't complain. Well, not too much. And at least I scored on dessert, which was homemade Boston cream pie and, if I do say so myself, perfectly luscious. But oh, the calories! Good thing I brought my Pilates video with me.

After dinner we sit in the living room with all the magazine pictures that Jenny and I have been tearing out spread across the coffee table. Beanie brought along even more that she's collected too. So, as we're sitting there amid this collage of every imaginable kind of bridesmaid dress, I began to feel a little overwhelmed. Almost dizzy. Or maybe it's the aftereffects of that rich dessert.

But as Jenny and Beanie go back and forth about whether the dresses should be on the shoulder, off the shoulder, or maybe strapless...not to mention whether they should be pastel colors or maybe black...or whether the dresses should be full length or tea length or even short...and on and on they go until I seriously can't stand it anymore.

"This is so impossible," I finally tell them as I flop back onto the sofa and clutch my head as if it's about to explode. "I'm sorry, but there are just too many options here."

"So what do you suggest?" asks Jenny. "You want to close your eyes and just randomly pick out a few that we can discuss?"

"The problem is, you still don't know what kind of a wedding you're having," Beanie says, as if she's suddenly become the wedding expert. "You don't know what it's going to be."

"I know where it's going to be," I tell her. "And even where the reception will be held." I've already told them my good news.

"But you don't even know what your dress is going to look like," says Beanie. She looks over at Jenny. "I can't believe that. I'm not even going with a guy and I totally know what my wedding gown will look like. Well, at least what I'd wear this year."

"But that's your thing," I remind her. "I'm not creative like that."

"But it's your wedding. You must have some idea."
Beanie looks frustrated.

"She's right," says Jenny. "You must have some idea
what kind of wedding you're going for. Like is it going to
be traditional, contemporary, creative, or—"

"Yeah, yeah," I say, waving my hand. "You already
read that list from 'Bride's' magazine to me, and like I
told you, those words just don't really mean anything to—"

"Wait a minute," says Beanie suddenly. "I think we're
going about this all wrong."

I want to say "duh" but know that would sound
pretty immature. So I just wait. And I can almost see the
wheels in Beanie's brain spinning.

"Okay, this is what I do when I'm trying to come up
with a new design." She points at me. "Are you willing to
do this with me, Caitlin?"

"Sure, whatever."

"Okay, first just close your eyes." She looks at Jenny.
"Let's all do it. Now just breathe deeply, okay? Really
relax and let everything we've been looking at sort of
drain out of you. Imagine that you're looking at a perfectly blank canvas and then just breathe deeply." She
pauses for a while, and I do this until I think I have a
blank canvas in my mind.

"Now I want you to think about your wedding day.
Think about how much you love Josh and how you're going
to feel on that day." She pauses again, and I almost feel
as if I'm being hypnotized, but I don't say anything. I just

go with the flow and try to think about that day in June. I imagine the sun shining and how happy I will feel.

"Now think about the location where you and Josh will say your vows. Just imagine the sanctuary, the guests sitting in the pews, the color of the wood and the carpet and the windows..."

And I can see it. I can really see it with flowers and candles, and suddenly I can even see a wedding party up there. It's like a photograph, only maybe a little blurry. But I really think I know what it is now, and I sit up and open my eyes and shout, "I've got it!" which makes Jenny jump—I think maybe she'd fallen asleep.

"What is it?" Beanie demands as she grabs a sketch pad and tosses Jenny a notebook. "Take notes, Jenny. And speak slowly, Caitlin, and use lots of description, okay?"

"It was like a vision," I begin. "I saw the church like you said, and I saw Josh standing up in front. He had on a simple black tux, not tails, and a white shirt and white rose in his lapel..."

"Good," says Beanie. "This is good."

"And the other groomsmen had on similar tuxes, only they had pale pink roses in their lapels. And then I saw the three bridesmaids. All beautiful brunettes with their hair worn up. And they had on pink—"

"Pink?" This comes from Jenny, and she's making a face. "Did you say pink?"

"Shh," says Beanie. "It's Caitlin's vision. Go on."

"Yes, the dresses were pink. But they were this beautiful pale shade of pink, and I could tell they were that heavy kind of satin I like, and they were tea length." I smile, proud that I noticed this. "The hem came down just a couple of inches above the shoes. They might've been longer in back, but not dragging on the floor. And they were a really simple style—"

"Okay, this is important," says Beanie. "Be specific."

"Right. The bodice had kind of a wide-open neck, graceful, you know? And there were straps. No, not straps; it was just the way the bodice was cut. It went to the edges of your shoulders and was sleeveless, like you'd have to wear a strapless bra, do you know what I mean?"

Beanie grabbed a photo of a peach-colored dress with shoulders like that.

"Yes, that's it. And oh yeah, you guys had on pearl necklaces and pearl drop earrings. Very elegant looking. The skirt was kind of A-line and fairly full at the bottom. Not fluffy full, but it wasn't narrow either. It just sort of flowed nicely from the bodice, all in one piece. Maybe they had princess seams, but I'm not sure. But the skirt looked full enough to dance in."

"I like that," says Jenny.

"Caitlin, this is great."

"And the sanctuary looked so beautiful," I continue. "There were white candles everywhere, and lots of green vinelike things trailing—"

"Like ivy?" suggests Jenny.

"Yes. That was it. And there were a few flowers but only in white and soft shades of pink. They seemed like lilies only smaller; I don't know for sure what they were."

"And your dress," Beanie says with enthusiasm. "Tell us about your dress."

I frown now. "I'm not sure."

"Didn't you see it?"

"Uh, no, I guess not. I think I was walking down the aisle. But I know that it was white and long."

Jenny giggles. "Helpful."

"That's okay, Caitlin. At least we know what the bridesmaids' gowns look like. That's what we really needed to nail tonight."

After a few minutes, Beanie turns the sketch pad toward me to show a gown that looks exactly as I described. "That's it," I tell her. "You're amazing."

"Good job describing it," says Beanie. "Now what?"

"Well, it sounds as if you're going to be pretty busy in New York," says Jenny. "You want me to see if I can track down these gowns?"

"That'd be great," says Beanie. "I'll keep my eyes open too. I'm sure we'll figure it out by June."

I am so relieved tonight. Okay, maybe I still don't know what my gown will look like. But I know it will be perfect, and I'm not the least bit worried.

Friday, December 30

Christmas was busy and lovely and romantic. Once again, Josh and I made the circuit, splitting our time between families and even taking time to go see Patty and Bob again. Patty even got us a special Christmas ornament to commemorate our "engagement" Christmas.

Josh really liked his cuff links and thought the JC initials were very cool. I told him my idea for having this on our wedding bands too. And he gave me a beautiful heart-shaped silver locket.

"I know you have that one from your dad, supporting your abstinence pledge," he said quickly. "And this isn't meant to replace it. But I guess I wanted you to have one from me as well."

The locket was engraved with "My Love Forever, Josh" on the back, and on the inside he'd put a tiny photograph of himself on one side and one of Jesus on the other. "I guess you have room for two men in your life."

I smiled and hugged him. "This is the best Christmas ever."

And it was. But then Christmas was over, and suddenly both Josh's mother and mine decided to go on the wedding warpath. Okay, maybe it wasn't exactly a warpath, because it seemed the two women were in cahoots. But it's like they thought they were going to get everything nailed before I went back to school.

Consequently, I have spent way too much time at florist shops and bakeries. I've seen the latest in men's formal wear and tried on enough veils to last a lifetime. But I know I'm a disappointment to both mothers since no real decisions were made.

Well, other than the tuxes. I did pick out a couple that looked like what I'd seen in my "wedding vision." And although Joy preferred the more formal evening-wear styles with tails—and I think she might've even gone for top hats and canes (okay, that's an exaggeration)—I tried to convince her that these would be more fitting with the bridesmaids' gowns.

"You've picked them out?" she said with surprise.

"Not exactly. But we nailed what they're going to look like, and Jenny and Beanie will be on the lookout."

Then she insisted I describe them to her, and as soon as I said the word "pink," she shuddered. "Surely, you don't want pink, Caitlin."

We had paused for a cup of coffee at this point, and my mother sat across from me suppressing a smile, since we'd already had the "pink discussion" too. So without saying anything I just nodded.

"But pink is so, so…" I could tell she was trying to pick a polite word. "Well, cliché."

Cliché? Now I hadn't heard that one yet. At least she hadn't said "infantile" or "childish" or even "Barbie," which was Chloe's first reaction. She's always made it clear that she's not a "pink" sort of girl.

"What about Pink the rock star," I reminded her, which made her laugh.

"Yeah, she's cool," she admitted.

But back to cliché. "What do you mean cliché?" I asked politely.

"Well, it used to be either pink or blue," she explained. "So predictable."

And so I attempted to explain my vision for pale pink, and after a bit, she finally got it too.

"That actually sounds rather elegant. Not at all what I was imagining."

I smiled. "Were you seeing bubble-gum pink with fluffy dresses and puffed sleeves?"

She seemed slightly embarrassed. "Yes, I suppose it was a bit like that."

Finally this week had come to a blessed end, and I'm so glad I can go back to school and focus my attention on things like classes and assignments and tests. All much less complicated than wedding plans. I wonder if there's some way a person can get college credits for planning a wedding. It certainly is a learning experience, not to mention draining.

Sunday, January 1

Josh and I got all dressed up, then went to this fancy dinner were we had a romantic, candlelit New Year's Eve dinner, cozying up in front of a fireplace and—NOT. Okay, a girl can imagine.

The truth is, we spent a crazy New Year's Eve with a bunch of hormonal high school students at the local roller-skating rink. Actually, it was fun. Josh had organized the event and it was limited to just our youth group kids. It was a way for high school kids to have fun in a somewhat controlled and alcohol-free environment. To get in, they had to have high school ID and be dressed like people from the fifties. Okay, for some of the guys it was just wearing a white T-shirt with their

sleeves and jeans rolled up. Like, what's up with that?
But some of the girls went all out with poodle skirts and
ponytails and all sorts of cool stuff.

I had a definite advantage since I'm still house-sitting
for my grandma, and she has a trunk full of funky
clothes from the fifties. I couldn't believe it when I found
what I'm guessing was a prom or bridesmaid dress—the
kind that Josh's mom had been imagining I was having in
my wedding. It was kind of this sick-looking Pepto-Bismol
pink, with all these ruffles and a huge skirt with layers
of netting to hold it out. (Although they'd gotten pretty
limp over the years.)

But I also found some hilarious pieces of costume jewelry—we're talking major rhinestones—and this funny
little pink hat with a net that comes over your eyes. I'm
sure they were never meant to go together. But I put
them all on, then sneaked into Grandma's makeup and
found this red lipstick called Fire-rod, and believe me it
was. And I was quite a sight to see. Josh practically split
a gut when he picked me up. He was driving the church
van and already had a load of kids in the back.

And okay, I know I'm a little old for this, but I had a
total blast hanging with these high school kids. Even
Chloe, Allie, and Laura were there—dressed like the
Supremes (although Laura's the only one who could really
pull it off), and they even did a couple of numbers that
were pretty convincing. It was a hoot. I don't know when
I've had so much fun. Maybe back in high school. But it
was a good reminder that we need to laugh and not

take life so seriously. I actually felt sorry for Jenny and
Beanie since they were at an "adult" New Year's Eve
party at Jenny's parents' house. Boring!

When midnight came around and we were all skating
to some romantic, crooning fifties tune with the sparkling
lights from a mirrored ball spinning all around us, Josh
caught up with me. And the next thing I knew, we were
kissing on wheels. Now I ask you, how many girls can brag
about that?

DEAR GOD, THANKS FOR LIGHTHEARTED, FUN
TIMES. PLEASE, HELP ME NOT TO TAKE LIFE TOO
SERIOUSLY. AND PLEASE BLESS THE NEW YEAR
AND ALL THE SURPRISES THAT LIE AHEAD. HELP
ME TO HEAR YOUR VOICE AND TO HONOR YOU
EVERY DAY. AMEN.

FIFTEEN

Thursday, January 5

It's great to be back into the normal routine of school again. I can't believe I'm saying that. But I guess since I got engaged, it feels more and more like my life's been turned upside down. Now, I'm not complaining. But it just feels as though I'm getting pulled in a lot of different directions. I'm glad this is my senior year. I couldn't imagine going through all this any earlier in the game. It would've been too much too soon. At least for me.

The night before I left home to return to school, my parents came over to my grandma's house to visit. Still practicing, I'd even baked an apple pie, and it wasn't too bad; although I think the crust was a little tough. Anyway, my dad said it was delicious, and my mom suggested I use more shortening next time. Then just as they were getting ready to go, my dad handed me something.

"What's this?" I asked as I looked at the small book.

"It's your wedding account."

"We thought you should keep track of your expenses," said Mom.

"We know you're good at maintaining a budget," he said.

My mom smiled. "And it's less confusing this way."

"I wish there was more in it." My dad sighed. "But it's the best we can do right now."

"Did you do the refinance?" I felt terrible, as if I'm the reason my parents are getting in over their heads.

"Yes. But don't you worry. It's the best thing we've ever done. Our interest rate is lower, and our monthly bills have been reduced so much that we're actually saving money."

"Really?"

Mom nodded. "It's true."

Then I flipped open the checkbook to the register and was surprised to find it was a lot more than I'd expected. "This is too much," I said quickly. "Really, I'm cutting corners wherever I can. I don't need this—"

"Look, Catie," said my dad. "It's barely half of what they say the average wedding costs."

"But they're crazy," I told him. "I know I can do this for less."

Mom nodded. "Good. Do it for less."

"Then I can return the savings to you?"

"No." My dad patted me on the back. "It's yours,

honey. Spend it all on the wedding or save it for your future. It's up to you."

"Wow." I looked at the figure again. I've never had this kind of money before. Not all at once.

"We know you'll do the right thing with it," my mom assured me.

"Thanks," I told them. Then I hugged them both. "I'll be careful with it."

And I plan to be careful. Not only that, but I found an article in the back of one of those wedding magazines. I'm sure they hid it in the back because they didn't want anyone to really read it. But I did. It was about ways to cut costs for your wedding. Ironically, I'd already done some. But now I'm determined to save as much as possible.

I mean, I want my wedding to be nice, but it's not like it has to impress anyone, well, besides Josh and me. And if we do this wedding for less, maybe we can use our savings for something good—like food for the kids in Mexico. Now, there's a real motivator when it comes to saving money. Every time I'm making a decision, I should measure the savings in rice and beans. Okay, I don't plan on announcing this to, say, the caterers, but it will definitely be going through my head.

Anyway, I'm back in school, and on Tuesday I enticed Jenny to go to coffee with Liz and me. And even though I could sense Liz's resentment at first (like "why did you bring HER along?"), it turned out okay. I'd told Jenny a little about Liz and her past with guys and Jenny just started opening up. And here's the kind of pathetic part—before we called it a night, both of my friends were ragging on me.

"Yeah, Caitlin's always been the <u>good</u> girl," said Jenny as she winked at me. "I mean, besides her abstinence vow, if she wasn't preaching at us to give up boys, she was out on the street saving orphan children."

"I didn't do that."

"I know just what you mean," said Liz with a twinkle in her eye. "I've heard that old I'm-saving-myself-for-marriage speech so many times that I almost know it by heart."

And then they actually started saying it (well, their version of it) together. I felt so stupid and slightly irked, but then suddenly I saw that they were only trying to get a rise out of me, and I started to laugh. Pretty soon we were all laughing and making up jokes for ways that girls could preserve their purity.

Okay, some of the jokes were pretty raunchy and gross—like why would a guy want to sleep with a girl who never shaved her armpits and chewed tobacco and bathed only at Christmas? But we were on a roll, and we thought we were pretty funny. Even so, I think the manager of Starbucks was seriously relieved to see us go. I'm just thankful he didn't call campus security to have us thrown out.

"Too much caffeine?" he said sarcastically as we were leaving.

"Too much testosterone?" Liz retorted in her most acidic tone. That's when Jenny and I just ducked our heads and bolted out the door. Oh, well.

Monday, January 9

This past weekend was the high school ski retreat. And despite my desire to get back to my college routines and what I define as "normal," I am so glad I took the time to go to this. It was a totally amazing time. And nothing like the last time that Josh and I were on a ski retreat together. The fact is, we never even kissed. Not once.

Instead, I spent my time with eleven high school girls who just totally won my heart. Of course, two of them were already dear to me. I was so pleasantly surprised when Chloe and Allie were among the girls in my cabin. It turned out that they're taking a short touring break and won't be back on the road until early February.

"We have to enjoy some of the high school experience," explained Chloe after I'd hugged them both.

And it was so cool having those two there. It's as if their presence took the spirituality factor of our small group sessions to a whole new level. To be honest, I think that Chloe and Allie could've done the whole thing without me. But like Josh said, he needed an "adult" along. Mostly I felt like I watched as these two shared from their hearts and really got girls to open up. Sure, I answered questions and told them about things like my little abstinence pledge (will I ever be known for anything besides that?), but it seemed to be Chloe and Allie who got these girls to thinking.

I met a girl who was relatively new to the youth group. Her name is Kim Peterson, and she was the quiet one in the group. She told me she'd just recommitted her life to Christ, but for some reason I was drawn to her immediately. Maybe it was her petite Asian good looks or her sweet spirit. But I could tell she was very intelligent, and she asked some very probing questions—some that we couldn't fully answer. But I was impressed with her maturity and I really hoped I could get to know her better.

Then Chloe and I were riding a chairlift together and she asked me how the wedding plans were coming and specifically about music. And I told her I hadn't lined anything up yet. "As far as the wedding goes, I'm just not sure," I admitted. "I want it to be kind of subdued and classic, you know?"

"Yeah, I can imagine that."

"Okay," I said, "Tell me if this sounds dumb...but I'd like to have 'Ave Maria'—not sung but played, and I was thinking maybe violin. Is that crazy?"

"No, I think it'd be beautiful."

"But isn't it a pretty difficult piece? Do you think I'd ever find anyone who could do it justice?"

Chloe got this big grin, and for a moment I actually got worried that she would offer to play this on guitar. Okay, I love this girl, but the last thing I want to see at my wedding is Chloe, complete in bridesmaid gown, up there blasting out "Ave Maria" on her electric guitar.

"She's in your cabin."

"Huh?"

"The person who can play 'Ave Maria' on violin."

"Seriously?"

She nodded as she got her snowboard situated to exit the chair.

"Who is it?" I asked as we both came off.

"Kim!" she shouted as she went flying down the slope.

Well, before the day was over, I discovered that not only was Kim a sweet and intelligent girl, she was probably the most gifted violinist within a hundred-mile radius. Maybe even more. Even so, she was very humble when I asked her about it.

"Do you want me to audition?" she asked.

"Judging by what Chloe and Allie say, I don't think it's necessary. But how do you feel about 'Ave Maria'?"

"I think it's beautiful."

"And you know it?"

"Sure." Kim smiled. "And I'd love to play it for you and Josh."

So there you go. I'm off trying to be a good high school counselor, and I discover a musician to play at our wedding. Go figure.

But then this weekend was just one of those amazing times when it felt like God was at work and the Holy Spirit was breathing on everyone. By our last "talk time" on Sunday morning, five of the girls in my cabin had recommitted their lives to Jesus and the other four were

more excited than ever about serving God. It was awesome. When it was time to go our separate ways on
Sunday, we all hugged each other and cried.

Oh yeah, the skiing and snowboarding was great too.
They had six new inches of powder on Saturday morning
and hardly any waiting time on the lifts. I mean, seriously, does life get much better than this?

But this weekend (and maybe the last one too) got
me thinking. The thing is, I'm seeing more and more how
well suited Josh is to youth ministry. His ability to deliver
a message that really hits kids right where they live,
and the way he reaches out to everyone is truly amazing. Not only that, but the way kids respond to him is
phenomenal. It's like he totally gets them and they
absolutely love him. And I've seen some great youth pastors in the past. Clay Berringer was unforgettably
awesome, and his life and death impacted me more
than anyone else I know.

But in some ways (and hey, I may be biased), Josh
reaches kids even better than Clay. Maybe it's because
Clay was so serious and intense, like he kind of overwhelmed us sometimes. But then who knew how short his
life was going to be? It's like he needed that kind of
intensity to accomplish all that he had to do. And I know
I will never forget that guy. But when I watch Josh inter-
acting with kids, or speaking up front to the group, well,
I'm just blown away at what a natural he is and how
much the kids trust and love him.

"He's the real thing," a girl named Cammie said to me. And I have to agree.

DEAR GOD, THANKS FOR THE FANTASTIC TIME WITH THESE GIRLS. THANKS THAT I AM HOOKED UP WITH A GUY LIKE JOSH WHO REALLY HAS A HEART FOR YOUNG PEOPLE. PLEASE, SHOW US THE DIRECTION YOU HAVE FOR OUR LIVES, NO MATTER WHAT IT MIGHT BE, AND HELP US TO FOLLOW YOU WHOLEHEARTEDLY WHEREVER YOU LEAD. AMEN.

Tuesday, January 10

Of course, I got my reality check—rather my wedding reality check—when I got back to my dorm and finally had time to open the package Josh's mom sent home with me on Sunday night. Naturally, I'd forgotten that I'd suggested that she might look into wedding invitations, since she seemed to know so much about this sort of thing. And that's just what she did.

The large manila envelope had about six different styles of very formal-looking invitations, complete with heavy embossing, pieces of pale-colored tissue paper and ribbons that tied and all sorts of goodies. The problem was, when I looked at the price list, I was stunned. I mean, each invitation cost as much as a very nice Hallmark card (which multiplied by three hundred, our current estimate, gets pretty spendy). Like I think I might be able to find a decent used car for this same price.

Anyway, instead of calling her up and asking who she thought was going to pay for this kind of nonsense, I began to do some research. Surely there were some options to these Cadillac invitations. And before long I discovered a very affordable alternative. Okay, so it wasn't embossed or beribboned or doesn't come with tissue. Hey, if she wants tissue, my grandma's got a lifetime supply of Kleenex in her hall closet, and I'm sure she'd be willing to donate a box or two.

My alternative was to have photocopied invitations. And while they may not have the elegant feel of those heavy, expensive ones—and what's that about anyway? Just a way to guilt unsuspecting guests into thinking they better spring for some costly wedding gift? I don't think so—I have no doubts that we can make our invitations into something special. So I played with some fonts and things on my computer. Before long Jenny started watching, and (after she teased me with, "Are you going to e-mail them to save on postage?") she actually got into the spirit.

"You know, I have a friend who's an art major. His name is Nick, and I might be able to get his help on this."

"Do you think he's affordable?" I asked.

"He's a student, Caitlin. How much more desperate does one get?"

So I printed out what I'd come up with so far and gave it to her. "Don't commit to anything," I told her.

Then I called my mom, I'm sure for moral support, and

she agreed with me that invitations do not have to cost a fortune. "I'll bet your dad could get them printed at work for the cost of the paper and ink."

So I asked her to check into it, and then I slipped Joy's envelope full of samples under my bed. And for the time being, I forget all about invitations.

Friday, January 13

Tonight was the first night of our marriage class at the church. Pastor Tony is taking seven couples, including us, through a marriage book. I felt a little funny since all of the other couples were already married (mostly newly-weds), and that made us look like real beginners. But as the class wore on, it became a real eye-opener when some of these people started expressing some of their problems. In fact, it was rather alarming when one couple actually got into a fight. Fortunately, it was time for a break, and Tony took them aside and reminded them of a few of the class rules.

"You okay?" Josh asked in a hushed voice as we went for cookies at the snack table.

"I think so." I poured myself some tea and tried not to stare at Tony as he counseled the feuding couple. "But that was pretty weird."

"Guess we should be glad we're taking this class before we tie the knot," he said as he picked up a cookie.

I smiled up at my beloved and wondered if we'd ever

have a fight like that—and in public. But then I'm sure all things are possible, and this couple may have gotten along perfectly well during their engagement period too.

Apparently, Tony's talk with the couple worked, but before the evening was over, it was clear that some of these marriages were already in trouble. Josh and I stayed to help clean things up and rearrange chairs so they'd be ready for youth group on Saturday night.

"Will you guys want to come back after tonight?" Tony asked after he'd told the last couple good-bye.

"I don't know," said Josh seriously. "I think you're scaring my girl. You keep this up, and she might refuse to marry me at all."

Tony laughed. "I'm sorry, Caitlin. I knew some of these couples were having troubles, but you never know what you're getting into until the can of worms is open."

"There's no denying that some of these couples need help," Josh said as he put the last chair in place.

"Well, I've already invited two couples in for private counseling," said Tony. "But there could be good reason for you kids to be here."

"And that would be...?" Josh eyed his boss carefully.

"For one thing, it's a good warning of what not to do." We both chuckled at this.

"And another thing is that you kids bring something healthy and wholesome to the table. These other couples made mistakes in their courtships and past lives that are still dogging at their heels now. Some of them are in second and third marriages. But you guys are a good example of how a marriage is supposed to begin. Of course, what happens after that is up to you." Then he slapped Josh on the back. "But so far, I'm impressed and I expect great things from you guys."

"What if we get into some big knock-down, drag-out fight in the middle of a marriage class?" I asked, even though I knew this was highly unlikely.

"Then I'll just take you aside and invite you in for private counseling the next day."

"So we're in good hands?" I smiled at Tony, knowing that we were.

"I'm just hoping you'll come back next week."

And so we promised him that we would. And who knows, maybe he's onto something. One thing is for sure, I don't want to have the kind of squabbles these guys are having one year from now. Maybe seeing it up close and personal is as good a lesson as anything. In the meantime, I'm going to be praying for these marriages. Especially the ones who lost it tonight.

I can't imagine how miserable it would feel to be that hurt by the man you've promised to stay with the rest of your life. It was bad enough to face the Josh and Jenny thing. But at least I'm moving forward. Even so, it's a little scary to think of how things could get out of hand in such a short period of married life.

DEAR GOD, I THINK I REALIZED MORE THAN EVER
TONIGHT THAT MARRIAGE IS A REALLY BIG DEAL.
NOT ONLY IS IT A LIFETIME COMMITMENT, BUT IT'S
SOMETHING WITH THE POTENTIAL TO MAKE YOU
TOTALLY MISERABLE IF YOU DON'T HANDLE THINGS
RIGHT. I NEVER WANT LIFE TO GO SOUR LIKE THAT
WITH JOSH AND ME. PLEASE, SHOW ME WHAT I
NEED TO KNOW TO BETTER PREPARE MYSELF TO
BE A GOOD LIFE PARTNER FOR JOSH. AND HELP
THOSE OTHER COUPLES WHO SEEM TO BE IN
SUCH PAIN. AMEN.

SIXTEEN

Wednesday, February 15

I guess I shouldn't have been too surprised
when, out of the blue, Josh showed up at my dorm yesterday (Valentine's Day). In fact, it's not even the first time
he's done something like this. About three years ago,
things didn't turn out so well for him. Fortunately, that
was then and this is now. But I'm beginning to think that
Josh is even more romantic than I am.

Even though he caught me off guard, I was totally
jazzed to see him! So were several other girls who were
coming home from class. He actually got some whistles
and hoots as he stood there waiting in the lobby. Of
course, he looked more handsome than ever in his dark
sweater and khaki pants. But with that gorgeous bouquet of red roses and killer smile, well, just let me say
that I was SO glad that he was here to see me! I
wasted no time snatching him up and then took him to

my room, where we scrounged around to find a vase, which actually was a water pitcher. Then realizing I was dressed in college grunge, I sent him downstairs to wait as I hurried to spruce up a bit.

"You're not wearing <u>that</u> are you?" Jenny said when she saw me about to leave. I still had on my jeans, but at least I had a fresh top, a dash of perfume, and some lip gloss.

I held up my hands. "What's wrong—?"

"Everything!"

And within mere minutes, Jenny put me through a makeover that could one day land her a cable TV show called "Five-Minute Makeovers for Frazzled College Students."

"Man, Jen," I said as I stared into the mirror. "I think you just found your calling."

"Well, it's Valentine's Day, you ninny. I couldn't let you go out with Josh looking like that."

Just as I was admiring my transformation, Liz walked in (she never knocks) and gave me an appreciative nod.

"You clean up pretty good, Caitlin."

Jenny had made me change into my pale blue cashmere sweater that my parents gave me for Christmas, along with a little black skirt and boots. Jenny even put my hair up in this sweet little twist, then loaned me a pair of her cubic zirconia earrings that look like the real thing. I already had on my Christmas locket and, if I do say so myself, I looked ready for an evening of romance!

"What are you guys up to tonight?" I asked, feeling a

little guilty for being the only one with a guy on Valentine's Day (what a switch!), since I knew that Liz had recently broken up with Leon.

"We're two beautiful babes doing the town without men," said Liz.

Jenny nodded. "Yeah, who needs 'em anyway." Then she handed me a large manila envelope. At first I thought it was a Valentine, and I felt bad because I hadn't gotten her one. But it turned out to be our wedding invitation, done in beautiful calligraphy, complete with a small RSVP card. Jenny assured me that both were an actual envelope size.

"He said it's all ready to photocopy. Just don't get the originals wet or the ink will run."

"That's nice," said Liz, looking over my shoulder.

"It's fantastic," I said as I admired the perfect letters. "How much do I owe this guy?"

Jenny waved her hand. "It was hardly anything. I already took care—"

"I can't let you pay—"

"That's enough from you," she said, "Don't you realize your prince is downstairs waiting?" She slipped the pages back in the envelope and handed it to me. "You better let him have a look at this."

So I thanked her and hugged them both, then dashed down to meet my prince. And we had the sweetest time. Josh thought ahead to make reservations at this Italian restaurant in the city, and it couldn't have been more perfect. By the time he brought me back to the dorm, I felt like a real princess.

Today it was back to the daily college grind. Naturally it's midterms and the weather is gloomy and gray. Still, it was nice to come back to my room and see those cheerful red roses as a reminder of last night's wonderful evening.

And this may sound lame, but I feel I'm entitled to a few fun dates. I mean, most girls go out all the time, but it's like I've been waiting forever for this part of my life to come. Still, I am so glad I gave up dating back in high school. It makes everything with Josh seem wonderful and new and exciting. I think that's how it should be. At least for me. Now I need to study for tomorrow's test.

Sunday, March 5

Last week had seemed longer than usual, and I was so ready to go home for the weekend. Although I wasn't ready to be confronted by both mothers (not at the same time, fortunately) over the fact that I have yet to find the perfect wedding gown. It's not as though I haven't been looking, but it's just that the ones I like are so expensive and yet even the pricey ones don't seem completely right either. I tried to explain to the "mothers" that I'm trying not to obsess about this. I'm trying to trust God to provide the right dress at the right time. But they were not getting it.

"You can't keep putting this off," my mom told me yesterday. "Your dress is important, and you need to figure it out." And then she insisted we go to a couple of the small local shops. "I already called them, and both assured me that they have some new gowns."

I tried to be hopeful and keep a positive attitude, but the "new" gowns didn't seem much different than any of the other ones I've seen.

"Maybe we should concentrate on veils," Mom suggested after I gave up on dresses. So we spent about an hour trying on veils, which I think was actually helpful. At least I know the styles I like now. But how can you pick out a veil when you don't even have a dress?

"Maybe the right veil would lead you to the right dress," my mom said as she held up her favorite choice, which was definitely not mine. Too princessy. Of course, I didn't tell her that.

"I think that's backward," I said. "Kind of like getting a set of tires before you get a car. What if they don't fit?"

She seemed to accept this, and we called it a day.

But on the previous evening, Josh and I had eaten dinner with his parents. Naturally the topic of my dress had come up right away, and I could tell that Joy was disappointed in me, although I assured her that Mom and I could get lucky.

"How about the bridesmaids' dresses?" she asked in a dismal tone.

"It's under control," I said. "Jenny met with a seamstress last week, and they even went fabric shopping and got what I think will be perfect. She'll start working

on the dresses as soon as she gets everyone's measure-
ments."

"That's a relief." Joy smiled. "How about shoes?"

"Jenny found the perfect shoes for the bridesmaids,"
I said. "And she faxed a picture to Beanie, and Beanie
approved."

"And we won't need to worry about Chloe, since her
opinions on bridesmaid shoes will be inconsequential." She
laughed. "I'm just glad she gave up wearing her Doc
Martens with every single outfit."

"It's part of her rock-star persona," offered Josh.

"That's right," said Stan. "And if anyone can pull off
that look, it's Chloe."

"And at least she's trying new styles," I said. "She's
really come a long ways since her Goth era."

And while I was glad we'd moved the conversation
from wedding dresses, I felt a little guilty that it was at
Chloe's expense. Fortunately, Josh and I had to "eat and
run" since it was marriage class night.

I'm actually glad that we're doing this class. It's
made me aware of a number of things I hadn't even
considered. Like when we took the compatibility quiz, I
was surprised at how different our tastes were about
certain things. Fortunately, we agreed on the things that
matter most—things like not getting into debt, when to
have children, religion, and politics.

But as Pastor Tony says, "It's the little things that
can get you. Things like one person who leaves their dirty
socks on the floor or the cap off the toothpaste."

Fortunately, both Josh and I are fairly neat. But Tony did mention that the division of household chores can really put stress on a marriage. "Times have changed," he said. "In most marriages, both partners work. It's not fair to expect the woman to put in forty hours a week and still carry the bulk of the household duties. Men today need to know how to do laundry or grocery shopping."

But here's what stuck with me the most: Tony said that the best marriages are not the ones where partners have a fifty-fifty agreement. As in, "You do your share and I'll do mine." He said that the Christian example of serving each other suggests that both partners should do 100 percent of the giving and helping. "The reason this works so well," he explained, "is that we usually can't do all that we think, and to constantly give 100 percent would be tough. But if you make that your goal and then hit only 75 or even 60 percent, you've still gone more than halfway, which doesn't leave a gap in the middle." I get that, and I'll try to keep it in mind when we're married.

DEAR GOD, HELP ME TO BE A 100 PERCENT GIVER
IN MY MARRIAGE. REMIND ME TO BE LIKE YOU AND
TO PUT JOSH AHEAD OF MYSELF. MOST OF ALL, I
PRAY THAT YOU'LL PREPARE BOTH OF US TO
ENTER INTO THIS MARRIAGE IN A WAY THAT
TOTALLY GLORIFIES YOU. AND BY THE WAY—IF
YOU'RE NOT TOO BUSY, COULD YOU HELP ME TO
GET THE WEDDING DRESS DILEMMA RESOLVED
BEFORE LONG? AMEN.

Thursday, March 23

It's been nice being home for spring break. Nice but busy.
Naturally both my mom and Josh's had lots for me to do
regarding wedding preparations. My mom had even made
a list. I wouldn't be surprised if Josh's mother had made
one too, but she never mentioned it.

She did, however, inquire on the status of the invitations. Now I was thinking, since they don't need to be sent
out more than a month in advance, what's the big hurry?
My guess is that she was more concerned about how they
would look. Josh had assured her several times that we
were both perfectly happy with the less-expensive direction we've taken. But he already warned me that his
mom keeps referring to our invitations as "wedding flyers,"
like maybe we plan to go tacking them onto all the power
poles in town.

On Monday I asked my mom, "Do you think we should

look into getting the invitations printed this week?" She'd
already spoken to my dad's secretary Mrs. Greenly, who
said it would be no problem to have them printed there.

"That's probably not a bad idea," said Mom. "How
about if I give Mrs. Greenly a call this morning and ask
when would be a good day?"

As it turned out, Mrs. Greenly felt that today was a
good day, and that if I was willing to supervise the copy-
ing, since I used to work there, I could have the copy
room—which includes copier, paper cutters, folders, and
anything else I might need—all to myself from noon until
three this afternoon. I'd already decided to use the
white card stock that the ad company orders by the
truckload. Not only is it the perfect weight, it couldn't be
cheaper.

Mom came along to help, and between the two of us, it
only took two hours to print, cut, and fold four hundred invitations. It was Mom's idea to do the extra ones, just in
case. And since Josh's parents haven't given me their complete guest list, it's probably not a bad idea. Besides,
they're so cheap that we can afford to throw them away.

"They look nice," said my mom, after the first ones
were all ready for their envelopes. But I could tell by
the way she said it that she wasn't totally convinced.

"They look nice, but they're kind of boring?" I finished
her sentence for her.

"I don't know..." She held up an invitation and studied it. "The calligraphy is beautiful, and I really like

that border of vines with the rose along the sides...but they're not very colorful."

I laughed. "They're black and white, Mom."

"Yes..."

"What's your point?" I asked, feeling slightly insulted by her criticism. "Do you think we should get out some felt pens and color—"

"That's it!"

I rolled my eyes. "Mom!"

"No, not felt pens. But what if I did just a bit of watercolor on it? Just to brighten it up."

I considered this. It's not as if I want these invitations to be boring, but I don't want them to look like second grade either. "I guess you could do a sample and show me," I finally said. "It's not like we have to use it."

"That's right."

So after we got everything printed and boxed and ready to go, I took my list of how much materials we'd used to the reception area (where I used to work), so I could write the ad company a check.

"Hi, Caitlin," said my old boss. "Congratulations on your engagement."

I smiled at her. "Thanks. I just printed the invitations." I showed her a sample and she nodded. "My mom has some ideas for sprucing them up."

"They're nice."

"Here's how much stuff we used." I handed her my list. "I didn't total it, but I figured you'd have a calculator."

She folded the paper and set it aside. "No charge," she said with a grin.

"No charge?"

"Nope. It's already been approved."

"Seriously?"

"That's right. You have a lot of fans here, Caitlin. It didn't take any arm twisting for them to decide to give you this."

"Wow, thanks."

I went to find my mom and tell her the good news. But here's what's strange. I have this checkbook with a pretty large amount of cash available, and so far I haven't spent a cent. How weird is that?

But here's the really fun part: After we got home, my mom disappeared up into her "mysterious" craft room, which she hasn't been letting me into. And in just a short while she returned, victoriously holding up an envelope.

"Open it up," she said.

I flipped it over to see a pale pink wax seal with a dove embossed into it.

"That's pretty," I told her as I popped open the still-warm seal and removed what I knew to be an invitation. But the plain white folded card looked a little more interesting, because it was tied with a narrow piece of pale pink satin ribbon with a dainty little bow in front. I untied the bow and opened the invitation to see that just a bit of color had been added—some faint green along the vine and a pale dot of pink on the rose.

Not only that, but she'd cut a piece of pale pink

tissue with some kind of fancy edge cutter that fit perfectly inside. I looked at Mom as if she were a genius. "This is incredible." I hugged her. "You're brilliant."

"And it didn't take long to do."

"But do you really have time to do this to all of them?"

"I don't see why not. They don't all need to be done at once. We still have at least six weeks before they even need to be sent."

"I can't wait to show Josh this," I told her. "And his mom! I mean, these look so special with hand-done calligraphy and hand-painted watercolors, and the ribbons—and all for free!"

"Well, I'll have to buy some more ribbon," she said. "But that's still not much to pay for such lovely invitations."

The next day, Josh's mother invited Mom and me to meet her in the city for lunch and shopping. "I've found something that you really must see," she told me in an excited voice. "It's the most wonderful new section of shops that recently opened close to the law office."

"Wedding dress shops?" I asked with great fear and trepidation. I really hate to lie, but I was ready to tell her anything (like I'm having liposuction surgery) to get out of another wedding dress nightmare with her.

"No, I already learned that lesson. These are some lovely design shops and florists and candy and whatnot. I think you might find some things for the wedding. There's one shop with the most amazing little chocolates wrapped in handmade paper that would make lovely wedding favors for your reception."

And since I could think of no good excuse and I didn't want to lie, plus this is, after all, my husband-to-be's mom, I finally agreed.

"It's not such a bad idea," said my mom, after I called her and invited her to drive me over there. "Just remember you don't actually have to buy anything, since I'm guessing these shops will be expensive. But we could get some ideas."

So we went into the city and met Joy at this little French restaurant for a light lunch. She hadn't seen the invitations yet, so I decided to get her reaction in person.

"You have to understand that they're not fancy, but on the other hand, they are virtually free. And the calligraphy was hand-done by an artist and—"

"Why not just skip the disclaimer and let me look at it," she said in a no-nonsense voice. So I handed her the envelope. I'd used my best handwriting to address it to her and Stan, and Mom had sealed it with wax. We both watched, and I think I may have held my breath as she opened it. She carefully examined everything inside, then looked up at us and smiled. "You did this for free?"

I nodded. "Do you think it'll be okay?"

"I think it's very nice. And it may not be as elegant as the embossed ones, but let's get real. Most people look at these invitations once, write the date on their calendar, and then throw them away."

So I was hugely relieved. But then we began looking at the specialty shops, and it wasn't long before I was overwhelmed with things like real flowers versus silk flowers, and beeswax candles versus dripless, and oh so many other things. Fortunately, my mom brought along a little notebook and was making notes. And I actually think she got some ideas too. So all in all the time wasn't a complete waste.

"Have you registered for your china and silver yet?" Joy asked as we were about ready to depart.

Now I knew this question was coming. I've heard about this practice from the brides' magazines. You go to some fancy store and pick out the patterns for your fine china and silver. Then you expect your poor unsuspecting wedding guests to fork over big bucks to buy it for you, have it wrapped, and bring it to your wedding. Call me old-fashioned or even crazy, but isn't that a little presumptuous, not to mention downright greedy? And whatever happened to people just buying the kind of gifts that they want?

Besides that, I just don't see Josh and me using fragile china and costly silverware down in the mission in Mexico. I may be weird, but I honestly think something more durable and inexpensive would be perfectly fine. Maybe even something from Target. Still, I haven't told a single soul about these wedding-renegade thoughts, and I hated to subject poor Joy to this now. Seriously, she must think I'm the cheapest, most boring future daughter-in-law on the planet.

"Uh, no," I told her, glancing at my mom and probably hoping for a little moral support.

"Well, you should start thinking about it." She looked at her watch. "It would be a fun thing for you and Josh to do together. Maybe you should have a date this week and see if you like the same things." She laughed. "I still remember how Stan and I couldn't agree on china. Finally, we compromised, but then it turned out that neither one of us really liked the dishes. I ended up giving them away a few years ago."

I nodded as if this made sense, but if anything it seems to confirm that my concerns about this are valid. So I spoke to Josh that same evening, and he couldn't see any sense in registering for something we had no intention of using. But when I told my mom this, she didn't exactly agree.

"If you're down in Mexico for a while, you might not use it at first, but you might want to use it someday." She got kind of a dreamy look. "I remember having special dinners with your dad, back before you were born. I'd get out the good china and light candles and it would be so romantic."

Okay, I guess that does sound somewhat appealing. I just don't know for sure. But I don't have to decide about this yet.

DEAR GOD, PLEASE, KEEP SHOWING ME WHAT IS
OR IS NOT IMPORTANT IN YOUR BIGGER SCHEME
OF THINGS. IT'S NOT AS IF I WANT TO BE A
SPARTAN AND LIVE A LIFE OF POVERTY. BUT I DO
WANT BALANCE AND BEAUTY AND MOSTLY YOUR
WILL IN MY LIFE. GIVE ME WISDOM TO MAKE ALL
THE DECISIONS THAT SEEM TO CONTINUALLY
COME MY WAY. AMEN.

SEVENTEEN

Tuesday, March 28

Once again, it was a relief to get back to my controlled life of school and classes. I think I really do like routines. I'd even missed our nightly weigh-in, which is still on track. I've lost ten pounds, and Jenny has put on about the same. We joke that we've been trading, like it comes off me, floats through the air, and winds up on her. Yeah, if it were only that easy.

But I must admit that already I'm feeling much better. I can fit back into my old jeans, and although I still have to lose that other five pounds, I'm in the best shape I've been in since high school. I guess I don't even care if I take off the last five or not.

But here's what's got me concerned tonight. Beanie called from New York this afternoon, and she's doing great. But she'd gotten this idea into her head, and I don't think there's anything I can do to dissuade her.

"Have you gotten your dress yet?" she asked after I'd barely said hello.

"No, I can't find anything that seems just right."

"Good."

"Good? I thought you were my friend."

"Good because I want to help you with this."

"Did you find a dress?" I asked eagerly, suddenly remembering that this girl is living on Fashion Boulevard.

"No, I haven't found one, but I'd like to make one."

"Oh, Beanie, that's a lot of—"

"Hear me out first. My spring project is supposed to be a wedding dress, Caitlin! Can you believe that?"

"I, uh, yeah..." Suddenly I was imagining myself walking down the aisle in some dramatic one-of-a-kind Beanie creation, and I was just not comfortable with that image.

"I want to do this for you, Caitlin. You've got to let me."

"But I don't know."

"Please. I already know what it's going to look like. Well, mostly."

"Can you tell me about it?"

"No, it has to be a surprise."

"Why?"

"Because I don't want you to mess with my muse."

"Your muse?"

"It's as if I could see this dress, Caitlin, kind of like when you saw the wedding. If I tell you about it, you might try to change something, and then it would vanish in a puff of smoke. And this is my term project; it has to turn out perfectly."

Well, what might be perfect for Beanie would not necessarily be perfect for me, and I was about to say forget it, but then I thought of something. "You have to create a wedding dress?"

"That's right."

"So, even if I didn't use it, you'd be designing it anyway?"

"Yes."

Now I was thinking maybe I could just go along with her plan and see how the dress turned out. It wasn't as if I'd found the right dress yet anyway. "Well, okay," I finally told her.

"I'm so glad. You're going to love it, Caitlin. I promise."

"And you know what the bridesmaids' dresses look like..."

"Yes, and yours will look perfect with them."

"This is going to be interesting." I was actually thinking more like scary, but I'm pretty sure I said interesting.

Okay, I hate to admit it, but I'm actually starting to worry about my wedding dress now. Sure, it would be wonderful if Beanie could design something I'd like, but it just seems highly unlikely. I mean, if I haven't found a dress after trying on dozens and dozens, how could she possibly make one that I'd like?

Maybe I'm just too picky. I'd like to think that I'd be content with whatever Beanie comes up with. She is my best friend, and I should be able to trust her with this.

But of all the pieces of this wedding, I guess I think the dress is the most important.

I can't even believe I haven't found the right one yet. Not only that, but I've been wondering about the one I let go. I mean, it's like I'm saving so much money on this wedding, I might've actually been able to afford it. But then how would I feel to be wearing that kind of money down the aisle?

Suddenly I envision a gown made of money. I'm sure if you took two thousand dollar bills and stapled them together, there'd be more than enough for a gown and train. But how would I feel wearing it? And why would wearing a dress that costs that much be any different? Oh, dear, I think I'm working myself into a panic. The only thing to do is pray.

DEAR GOD, I AM REMINDED OF HOW I PUT ALL THESE WEDDING PLANS, INCLUDING MY DRESS, ON YOUR ALTAR. AND IT SEEMS IT'S TIME FOR ME TO DO THIS AGAIN. REALLY, EVERYTHING HAS BEEN WORKING OUT SO PERFECTLY THAT IT SEEMS NOTHING SHORT OF MIRACULOUS. I TRUST YOU WITH MY DRESS NOW. I WILL NOT FREAK ABOUT IT. I KNOW IT'S ONLY A DRESS, BUT I ALSO KNOW YOU LOVE ME AND WANT WHAT'S BEST FOR ME. PLEASE, HELP ME TO WAIT PATIENTLY ON YOU. AMEN.

Saturday, April 8

It figures. Both my mom and Josh's mom are alarmed that I plan to wear Beanie's class project down the aisle. I wish I hadn't even told them. It's not that they don't think Beanie can make a perfectly nice wedding gown. They just feel the chances of me liking it will be like winning the lottery. Even Jenny is skeptical. Josh seems to be the only one who's fairly laid-back about it. Finally, I had to ask him why that was.

"I trust you, Caitlin."

"You trust me?" I studied his face. "But Beanie's the one making the dress."

"Yes, but if you agreed, then you must feel confident she can pull this off. And so I trust you."

"But what if it ends up being some strange-looking concoction with bobbles and butterflies and a fifty-foot train?"

He smiled. "You'd still be beautiful."

And so I figure if Josh is okay with this, I can be okay. After all, I did commit this to God. Probably the best thing would be to put it out of my mind. Even so, I did call Beanie last night. I told her it was because I wanted to know what I should do about the veil.

"What do you want to do?" she said sleepily, and suddenly I remembered she was on east coast time and I'd probably awakened her.

"I'm not sure."

"Well, I have a veil designed that goes with the

dress. But if you have something else picked out..."

"No, I haven't really seen any that I like that well."

"Good."

"Sorry to wake you up, Beanie."

"That's okay." Now there was a long pause, and I almost wondered if she'd fallen back asleep. "Just trust me on this, Caitlin," she said in a tired voice.

"I'm trying to. But you have to remember this is going to be one of the biggest days of my life. Maybe the biggest. This dress is a huge deal."

"I know. Just trust me."

So I told her that I would and to go back to sleep, then I hung up. And really, I know she won't let me down. At least not on purpose.

But I don't need to keep thinking about that. Here's a totally cool thing that happened today. Josh drove me out to see his grandma's farm. And while it's not a real farm with crops and animals, it's a sweet little place in the country with outbuildings and picket fences and chickens that lay real eggs and the most incredible flower gardens. I've never seen anything like it.

"You must really have a green thumb," I told his grandma. "These flowers are amazing."

"It's been a good year for the perennials."

Now to be honest, I don't know a perennial from a tulip, but I just nodded. "My mom grows a few flowers in our backyard, but nothing like this." We were cutting a selection of blooms for me to take home and enjoy, but the bouquet just kept getting bigger and bigger. "I guess that's enough," I finally said when the coffee can I was putting them in became full.

"Now that's a pretty picture," Josh called as he and his grandpa came our way.

"Here comes the bride," sung his grandpa.

"Wouldn't that be a pretty bridal bouquet." Josh leaned over to smell the colorful flowers.

"It's a little bright for a wedding," I told him. "I just wanted something cheerful to take back to school with me tomorrow."

"That ought to brighten your room," Grandma Brown said as she adjusted her straw hat to keep the sun out of her eyes. "The beauty of flowers is that they can create whatever sort of mood you like. They can be perky and cheerful, or quiet and respectful, or elegant or sweet..." She smiled. "It's all in the way you arrange them."

"Grandma Brown has won a lot of blue ribbons for flower arranging," said Josh. "And she used to teach classes too."

"Oh, Joshua, don't brag." But it was easy to see she enjoyed it.

"Maybe I should talk to you about my wedding flowers. I mean, I sort of know what I want, but I don't even know what they're called." Then I began explaining to her about my wedding vision and how I saw what I thought was ivy, and that I'd imagined some delicate white flowers, but I had no idea what they were.

So we sat my flowers in the shade, and she took me

around and showed me what they might possibly have been. As we walked, she cut several strands of ivy growing over one of her sheds, and then, like an expert, she cut several smaller white flowers and tucked them into it. "Something like this?" she asked.

I had to blink in amazement as I nodded. "Something exactly like that."

"Well, this would be the simplest thing to put together," she said. "No sense in your paying a florist to do this." She nodded to where the ivy was growing. "And I've been meaning to cut back that ivy before it swallows my whole shed. I guess I could wait until June."

"Really?" I asked her. "You'd do that for me?"

"Of course, honey. Flowers are my life. Nothing I'd rather do than put some together for your wedding. But are you sure that's all you want?" She looked around her garden. "Goodness knows this place will be nothing but blooms by the end of May. We'd have enough to do all sorts of things."

"But it's such an imposition."

"Not at all. I have a little garden club that would probably love to help."

I turned to Josh with wide eyes. "What do you think?"

"I think there'd be nothing sweeter than having Grandma Brown's flowers at our wedding. But are you sure?"

"I've never seen florist's flowers that were any prettier than these," I said. "I just don't want to impose—"

"Not another word," said Grandma Brown. "This is going to be a delight."

As Josh and I drove back to town, I told him how amazing it was that things just kept working out. "You know what I think," I said suddenly.

"That you're marrying the right guy?"

"Well, yes, I definitely think that. But you know what else I think?"

"What?"

"I think we have a divine wedding planner."

He laughed. "God as the wedding planner."

"It's true. It's like things just keep falling into place. At this rate, I almost expect a cake to fall from the sky."

"Then it would look like a pancake," said Josh.

"You know what I mean."

"Speaking of cake, do you think it could be something besides plain old white on the inside? Like maybe chocolate?"

"I don't know why not."

"Do you know where you want to get it yet?"

"I know where I don't want to get it," I told him. "Not from Le Fountine."

"Too expensive?"

"I'll say. I mean, sheesh, it's only a cake. But I don't want one from the grocery store either. I know I'm trying to stretch our pennies, but I think we can do better than that. Besides, I want it to taste good."

Saturday, April 22

I had my first official "wedding gown" fitting today. But this is how it worked. Beanie had FedExed the "dress" to Aunt Steph, and then Steph invited a seamstress friend named Dorothy over to her house to check and make sure it was fitted correctly. But before I could try on the dress, I was blindfolded.

"Why?" I asked.

"Beanie's instructions," Steph said as she securely tied the blue bandanna over my eyes. "No peeking either."

And then she and Dorothy went to work slipping something soft over my head and pinning it here and there. But I could tell by touching the fabric that it was all wrong. Still, I didn't say anything. I just stood there and did what they told me to do, thinking that as soon as they finished, I would borrow my mom's car, take a fast trip to the city, and purchase the dress that I'd allowed Joy to return. I just hoped that it was still there.

"Are you okay?" asked Steph after the "dress" was finally removed and Dorothy had left.

I shook my head, holding back the tears.

"What's wrong?"

"Everything," I said. "The dress—I know it's wrong—I can feel it. The fabric feels like—"

"Oh, Caitlin," said Steph quickly. "I should've told you. That's not the actual dress."

"It's not?"

"No, of course not. That's a model Beanie will use for

a pattern for the real dress. She used plain cotton for the fabric; I think she called it a dummy."

"Oh." But I felt like the dummy.

"She just needed to know it fits perfectly before she sews the real thing."

I nodded. "Yeah, I get it now." Then I looked closely at Aunt Steph. "But can you just tell me this? Do you think it's pretty? Do you think it's going to be okay?" Now her expression was absolutely no help. It was a cross between uncertainty and concern.

"I'm sure it's going to be beautiful," she finally said. "Really, it's impossible to tell from the dummy dress. But it did fit you nicely."

I sighed. "It's just so hard not knowing."

"I know, sweetie. But trust Beanie; she's a pro."

"I'm trying to, but I'm still wondering if I should get a backup dress, in case something goes wrong."

"I don't know what to tell you." Then Steph looked as if she'd just remembered something. "Oh, yeah. Beanie did say to tell you she'd found the perfect shoes, and I think she was going to stick a picture of them in the box." She was already going through the box until she finally found it. "Here it is."

And I'll have to give Beanie this: The shoes were beautiful. "Wow."

"Those are gorgeous," said Steph. "If that's any indication of how great the dress is going to look, I wouldn't be worried if I were you."

And so I'm keeping that picture of the shoes on my

desk as a visual reminder that the dress is probably going to be just fine. And if not, well, at least my feet will look great.

> DEAR GOD, ONCE AGAIN I PLACE ALL THE DETAILS OF THE WEDDING INTO YOUR HANDS. I KNOW YOU CARE ABOUT ME AND MY WEDDING. I ASK THAT YOU WORK THINGS OUT AND REMIND ME TO PUT MY TRUST IN YOU. THANK YOU FOR YOUR PERFECT PEACE IN THE MIDST OF WHAT COULD BE PREWEDDING MADNESS. YOU TOTALLY REIGN! AMEN.

EIGHTEEN

Thursday, May 4

I can't believe it's already May. But these last few weeks have been so busy with classes, addressing invitations (which were just sent), and making more and more decisions that the time has really flown. And now I'm slightly freaked that my wedding is less than a month away. How can that be?

Mom and Aunt Steph have pretty much taken over the wedding decoration operation. They understand what I want (lots of white candles, ivy, and white and pale pink flowers), and I'm trusting that they really get it. And Mom's made it perfectly clear that the craft room is off-limits. As a result, I've continued to stay at my grandma's for the weekends, even though she's been home for a couple of weeks now. But she seems to enjoy my company, and I think she's a hoot. Plus, it keeps me away from my house where Mom and Steph are always hiding things whenever I show up.

Now I'm not sure how I should feel about all this secrecy. Is it because they're afraid I won't like what they're doing? And if that's the case, shouldn't I be a little concerned? Or is it that they simply want to surprise me? I just can't say, but I know that they like to tease me sometimes. Like last weekend when Steph said, "You should see the napkins your mom got for the wedding. Wow, they are <u>really</u> pink."

"Really pink?" I asked.

"Well, more magenta, I suppose. But hey, it was a good deal."

"Mom?" I felt my eyes getting big.

Mom thought this was great fun and played right along. "And then I found this great sale on candles at the craft store. Of course, they were leftover candles from Christmas, so I got them for practically nothing."

"<u>Christmas candles and magenta napkins?</u>" I knew they were stringing me along me now, but still.

"The Christmas candles are just basic white tapers," my mom assured me. "A nice shade of white and they're dripless."

"And the napkins?"

"Pale pink." She grinned. "The truth is, they ordered the wrong ones and when I opened the box they really were magenta. But the lady straightened it all out, and we have pale pink now."

"Do you think it's going to be too much pink?" I said suddenly. "I mean, I don't want it to look like a five-year-old girl's birthday party."

"I actually think that pale pink looks quite elegant," said Steph.

"How do you feel about balloons, Caitlin?" asked my mom.

"Balloons?" Now I wasn't sure if she was serious or not.

"Not very many. But I thought they might be fun at the reception. The lady at the craft store showed me how pretty the pale pink goes with the silver, and I thought maybe..."

I considered this. "You know, I think I'll just trust you with this."

And that's how it's been about a lot of things. Trust. Mostly I am trusting God and reminding myself that while this day is important, it's only <u>one</u> day. It's the marriage afterward that really counts. I know some people think I'm being way too laid-back. Like when I decided on the cake. One of my mom's coworkers had gotten a birthday cake from a new little bakery on the edge of town, and Mom told me how all of the teachers just went nuts over it.

"But I thought you said that teachers would eat anything," I reminded her.

"No, it was really good. And you still haven't ordered one yet. I think we should go check it out." And so Mom and I did. And although the exterior of the bakery didn't look like much, the interior was clean and bright, and the woman working there (also the owner) was knowledgeable and helpful and even let us sample several different kinds of cake. And then I looked through her binder notebook full of photos of cakes she'd made in the past. I was blown away. "These are beautiful."

"Thanks." She smiled. "We used to run a bakery in the city, but we're trying to slow our lifestyle down. Unfortunately, it's been a little too slow. By this time of year, I'm usually completely booked for wedding cakes."

"So, I'm lucky."

"I'll say." She laughed. "Most brides-to-be have their cakes ordered six months in advance."

My mom gave me "the look," and I just shrugged. "I've been kind of busy." But then I picked out a cake that I really liked and asked if she could make the roses a really pale pink. "Almost white," I told her. "I'd like the cake to look as if it's almost completely white."

"Sounds pretty," she said as she made notes.

"And can we have one layer in chocolate, one in lemon, and one in white?"

"No problem."

And just like that we were done and out of there. "Thanks, Mom," I told her. "You were right."

She smiled. "See, mothers do know a thing or two."

I laughed. "Hey, Mom, the older I get the smarter you seem."

"I was just thinking the same thing about you, honey. And I admire that you're not getting stressed about all the details. We could all learn something from you."

I don't know about that, but I am somewhat reassured to know that I probably won't be some grouched-out, falling apart, frazzled bride on June 1. My plan is to be as cool and calm as possible. I want to be ready to enjoy the day as much as I hope my guests will. I'm hoping Josh will do the same. After all, it's supposed to be a fun day—not a stressed-out picture-perfect affair that's only meant to impress people.

Speaking of not impressing people, Josh and I made the china and silver decision. And it was no. Of course, neither of our mothers was overly thrilled. Then Josh and I went to Target (otherwise known as Tar-jay with a French accent) to look at some more practical dishes and things. And what do you know? They actually have a bridal registry there. And feeling a bit silly, not to mention greedy, we went through the store and listed every item that we thought would be useful for our "household."

But here's the funny thing: We won't even have a "household" for a while. I suppose we could take a few things down to Mexico, but I have a feeling that most of our gifts will go into storage until the end of the summer. But we'll figure it out. But at least we've in agreement. We're both committed to spending a full summer in Mexico and then seeing what God has for us after that. I guess this is what you call living by faith.

Of course, Tony's made it clear that he doesn't want to lose Josh, and that he'll still have a full-time position for him in the fall (another seminary student will fill in during the summer). But neither Josh nor I know for sure what comes next. Mostly I need to focus on school, finals, graduation, and this wedding. I don't even know where we'll be for the honeymoon, but Josh assured me he's handling it. More room for trust.

Saturday, May 20

What a day this has been. After cramming all last week and taking finals this week, as well as trying to get all my ducks in a row to graduate next weekend, I was totally exhausted by the time Josh picked me up at the dorm last night. I actually slept all the way home, and I felt bad because I know Josh wanted to talk. Then I slept in this morning until nearly noon and didn't do much until I finally showered and dressed in time to be picked up by Josh at five-thirty. He was all apologetic that we only had about an hour to eat dinner.

"I just wanted to spend a little time with you," he said. "If it wasn't for this youth group thing tonight—"

"It's okay. My mom wants me to come over tonight to help with some of their wedding goodies anyway." I laughed. "I can't believe they're actually going to let me see something. It's like everything's been all top secret over there."

Then Josh dropped me off at my parents' at a little after seven, but I thought it was odd to see so many cars parked in our neighborhood. Still, he acted like it wasn't so unusual, although he did have this little twinkle in his eye.

You guessed it; I went inside to discover about forty of my female friends and family waiting for me, the guest of honor, to come to my wedding shower. But here's the best part—Beanie was there! I just broke down and cried when I saw her sitting on the sofa next to Jenny. I'd been feeling so bad that she's been so far away—and I suppose I've been wondering about my dress too.

I was blown away by the shower and all the lovely gifts. Of course, lots of jokes were made about how Josh and I would really need some of these items down at the mission in Mexico.

"But we have the rest of our lives," I reminded them. "I'm sure we'll figure it out and get settled down eventually."

"I hope so," said Joy. "I don't really like the idea of my grandchildren being raised down in Mexico."

"Speaking of grandchildren," Jenny said as I broke a ribbon to open a box. "There's another one." Someone made up this silly rule that for every ribbon you break at your bridal shower, it means you're going to have that many babies.

"That's seven kids so far," Beanie said as she collected another bow to put onto my rehearsal dinner "bouquet," which consists of all the wedding shower bows made into one colorful bunch.

All in all, it was a wonderful night, although I'm not sure if I actually visited with everyone there, but I tried. I know I'm still pretty worn out from the past couple of weeks. I'm looking forward to having some downtime between graduation and the wedding. Okay, at least a day or two.

Sunday, May 21

I hadn't wanted to ask Beanie about the wedding dress last night. I mean, what if she hadn't been able to finish it, or something had gone wrong? I didn't want to be a blubbering bride-to-be at my own shower. Talk about putting a damper on things. But I did ask her this morning at church.

"So how's the dress coming?" I say in this slightly hesitant voice, like I'm not sure if I want to hear the answer.

Her face is blank, but she says it is fine.

"By the way, how did you get to come home this early? I thought you had finals next week too."

"Two of my classes were graded by my term projects, and I was allowed to take the one final early when I explained my circumstances."

"Circumstances?"

"You know, that I was your maid of honor and everything."

"They let you leave for that?"

"Well, that and they understood about the wedding gown."

"Understood?" Now something about this is making me nervous, but it's too late to attempt to extract any more information from her, because Pastor Tony is already at the pulpit.

But as soon as church is over, I corner Beanie. "Look, I've really been trusting you on this, but do you realize it's less than two weeks until the wedding, and I have no idea what my wedding gown looks like, or for that matter, if I even have one?"

She grins and with raised brows says, "So, maybe you'd like to see it?"

We arrange to meet at high noon at my parents' house, since my mom is eager to see it too. As I wait for Beanie to get there, I am so nervous I actually put on a fresh layer of antiperspirant. She'd already told me, through e-mail, that I would need a strapless bra for this dress, and I had it on along with the proper hose (a beautiful pair of nude-colored, lace-trimmed thigh highs that Beanie had also recommended). And as I sit in my mom's bedroom, wearing her chenille bathrobe over this, I actually pray:

DEAR GOD, PLEASE, LET THIS DRESS WORK OUT. AND IF, FOR SOME REASON, I HATE WHATEVER IT IS THAT BEANIE'S CREATED, PLEASE, PLEASE, PLEASE, LET ME CONTROL MY EMOTIONS AND NOT ALLOW THIS TO HARM OUR FRIENDSHIP IN ANY WAY. I KNOW THAT YOU WILL PROVIDE A DRESS FOR MY WEDDING, AND I PUT ALL OF MY HOPES AND EXPECTATIONS ONTO YOU. AMEN.

And then I take several deep breaths. The next thing I know Beanie is coming into my parents' bedroom with a large garment bag. "You ready for this?" she asks.

I nod without speaking. I'm not even sure if I can speak.

"Okay. But do you mind if I have you close your eyes until you have it on?"

I nod again. Still speechless. I suppose I feel a little like the lamb on her way to the slaughter. But at least this isn't my wedding day. At least I will have time to sort this all out. With my eyes closed I feel the gown being lowered over my head and I must admit that the weight and the layers of fabric feel good. And I can tell as she zips up the side zipper and fastens some hooks that the fit is perfect, and so far the dress is quite comfortable. Although I don't know that comfort is necessarily a good sign, since the dresses I liked most weren't usually the most comfortable.

"Don't open yet," she warns. "I want to get the shoes and the veil."

So I stand there waiting and praying. Finally, she has me all set and turns me around, I feel sure, so that I am facing the mirrored doors on my parents' closet. "All right," she says in a nervous voice. "Open."

Well, I am just stunned. I cannot believe my eyes. And before I can say anything, I am crying, sobbing actually.

"Are you okay?" asks Beanie, and I can tell she is scared. "Is it all—?"

"It's awesome!" I tell her between sobs. "It's amazing. It's a miracle." And then we hug, and I can see that she is crying too.

"I got an A-plus on it, and everyone at school thought it was fantastic."

Then my mom comes in, and she starts crying too. "Oh,

Caitlin, it's perfect!" She turns to Beanie with wide eyes. "You are a wonder, Beanie."

"She got an A-plus," I tell her as I wipe my eyes and take time to more carefully examine the most beautiful dress I've ever seen.

The bodice fits me like a glove and is cut similar to a strapless gown, but it has these sheer gossamer-like pieces that gracefully go over my shoulders, kind of off the shoulder like the bridesmaids' dresses. But the incredible part is how the bodice is beaded with all these tiny pearly-looking beads. The pattern is delicate and yet classic, and really, if someone told me that angels in heaven had designed this dress, I would believe it. That's what I tell Beanie and she cries even harder. "I was praying the whole time," she tells me.

And the skirt is perfect too. It's made of the same heavy weight satin that I like, but it doesn't feel heavy or bulky as it gracefully flows to the floor. And instead of a train, which I frankly don't get, it is just a little longer in the back—very elegant looking. Even the veil is perfect. And of course, I knew that I already loved the shoes.

"I feel like Cinderella," I tell Beanie and Mom.

"You're going to be a beautiful bride." Mom hugs me again. "I'm so proud of you."

To say I am feeling hugely relieved is a total understatement. I am feeling ecstatic and blissful and like I am really living out my wedding dream.

DEAR GOD, THANK YOU! THANK YOU! THANK YOU
FOR YOUR FAITHFULNESS TO ME. I KNOW THAT
THE PERFECT WEDDING DRESS IS REALLY A TINY
THING IN THE GLOBAL SCHEME OF THINGS, BUT I
AM FOREVER GRATEFUL THAT YOU INSPIRED
BEANIE TO CREATE THE PERFECT ONE FOR ME.
YOU ARE MAGNIFICENT! AMEN.

NINETEEN

Wednesday, May 24

Josh was too busy to drive me back to school today, and I totally understood. Fortunately for me, Jenny's mom was driving her back, so I caught a ride with them. And I tried not to feel bad when Jenny's mom helped her pack up all her stuff and load it into their car and leave.

"I don't see why you want to stick around here," Mrs. Lambert said as they got the last load. And the truth is, I don't either, but then I know there's not room in the Lambert SUV for both Jenny's and my stuff. And since my mom's busier than ever with the last of the school-year activities with her second graders and my dad was swamped at work, I will simply bide my time as I carefully pack up my things. My plan is to just hang out here on campus until Saturday and the graduation ceremony, before I totally check out of this place for good.

"It's okay," I told her. "It might be nice to have a couple of days without anything much to do."

"I'd think you'd have plenty to do with your wedding in just over a week."

I smiled at her and noticed that Jenny was giving me the "Sorry, but this is my mom," look. Then I said, "It's really amazing at how little there is to do right now. Everything seems to be falling right into place."

And it really is. I looked over my list of things to do and somehow they all seemed to be under control. Even the music for the reception was covered. Chloe asked me a few weeks ago if we planned to have a live band.

"No," I told her. "Don't tell me you're offering. And if you are, forget it. I want you girls to just relax and have fun during our reception." I knew they would be leaving for their big summer tour on the Monday afterward, and there was no way I'd let them play.

"I wasn't thinking of Redemption," she told me. "Although we might have a little surprise for you. But there's this Christian band over in Mercer, and they've been trying to get us to listen to them. I've heard their demo, and they're really good. I told the leader that if you were willing, we could listen to them at your reception. Of course, they'd have to play for free."

I had to laugh. "No way! Are you kidding?"

"No. And Josh heard the demo and thinks they'd be great."

And so I listened to the demo and I agree. As a result, we're getting live music for free. "Don't worry,"

Chloe assured me. "These guys are totally jazzed to do this. For them to be heard by two of the hottest Christian rock groups—"

"Two?"

"Oh, yeah. I invited Jeremy to be my, well, not date exactly, but you know..."

So not only will Redemption be at our wedding, but the leader of Iron Cross too. That's quite a break for this new band, and I don't even feel bad that they're doing it for free. Also, I'm sure it'll be quite a show. Yeah!

It really seems like everything is pretty much under control. And I know I should use these next couple of days to just kick back. And I plan to, but I can tell it's not going to be easy.

Friday, May 26

I was right. It wasn't easy. The first night that I was alone in my dorm room, I had a nightmare—about Josh. I dreamed that he was cheating on me with someone (thankfully not Jenny), and I guess I never actually saw her face. But oh, it hurt so bad—just like it was really happening. I woke up sobbing and almost called Josh, but it was only five in the morning.

Of course, I told myself it was ridiculous and that Josh would never do that to me, but I was haunted by it all day on Thursday. I kept praying and trying to think about other things, but it wouldn't go away. As a result, I have been plagued with these awful doubts. What if I am doing the wrong thing? What if Josh really doesn't love me? What if our marriage is destined for failure? Arggh!

In desperation, I called Liz. We'd missed our Tuesday coffee time, since I hadn't come back to school yet. And okay, I realize it was probably a little crazy to call someone like Liz when I'm freaking out over Josh's fidelity or lack thereof. I mean, Liz is totally off guys right now, since she did discover that Leon (who seemed so nice) had actually cheated on her after all! But I called her without really thinking this through. I mostly just wanted someone to talk to.

She laughed when I told her about my dream. But not in a mean way. She laughed like she thought I was being ridiculous. "You're just having a prenuptial attack of nerves," she said as if she were the expert. "People do this all the time. It's your subconscious way of preparing yourself for what lies ahead. Like pregnant mothers dream that they have a baby that they're neglecting or abusing. It doesn't mean that's going to happen."

"Seriously?"

"That's my take." She grinned. "And I am a philosophy major."

"Now there's a degree that's going to take you places," I teased.

"Yeah, yeah, O'Conner...you should talk."

So we talked some more and laughed, and I realized that Liz was, after all, the perfect person to call. More than that, I realized that even though she's not a believer (yet!) she has a good heart and is a true friend. And I almost wish that I'd asked her to be a bridesmaid, but at least she's going to be on hand helping with the guest book and gifts. She didn't even make fun of this "job" when I asked her. She told me she'd be honored. Now really, who would've thought, back when I was a freshman, that Liz Banks would be managing the guest book at my wedding? Life's funny.

And so I told myself that my silly dream was just a case of the prenuptial jitters and best to be ignored. However, I did call Josh and tell him a little about my dream. He assured me that cheating on me was the furthest thing from his mind. And I believe him.

But this morning, Liz called and asked me how I was doing. I think she was really concerned.

"I'm feeling better," I told her. "Your advice really helped."

"So what are you doing today?"

"Just sitting around, looking at my packed boxes and wishing I had a good book to read."

"Have you done any shopping for the honeymoon yet?" asked Liz.

"Shopping for the honeymoon?"

"Yeah, silly. Don't you want to look hot for your hubby?"

"That's not such a bad idea."

"Well, I just happen to have my friend's car today. Do you have any money?"

I laughed. "Sure. With all that I've saved on this wedding, I'm loaded."

"What better way to spend some dough than for your honeymoon!"

And although Liz and I don't agree on everything, I have to think that this girl's got a lot of good sense. She picked me up, and we shopped until we literally dropped. But am I ever ready for the honeymoon now. I just wish I had a little bit of a tan started.

DEAR GOD, THANK YOU SO MUCH FOR LIZ! PLEASE
BLESS HER AND CONTINUE SHOWING YOURSELF,
YOUR LOVE, AND YOUR GRACE TO HER. I KNOW
THAT IN TIME SHE'S GOING TO GET YOU. AMEN.

Sunday, May 28

It's funny. After looking forward to my graduation all year, I am so glad that it's finally over. I suppose the wedding plans have overshadowed it a bit, but then I don't think there's anything quite as boring as a graduation ceremony. Seriously, I can't even believe that people are willing to sit and watch it. But then it's mostly just parents, and after all their hard work to put you through school, well, I suppose they deserve a little celebration—and maybe a little nap as they listen to all the same old speeches again and again. Sigh. At least it's over with, and I have my degree in hand and am ready to move on. Oh, I'm not saying that I'm finished with school forever. I may want to go back someday. But not for a long time.

Monday, May 29

I went out to see Patty and Bob today. Josh couldn't come, but I didn't mind going alone. Patty wanted me to make some decisions about where things should be during the reception. We've rented tables and chairs and whatnot, and Josh will have some guys from youth group do the setup, but Patty thought we should make them a little map.

I hadn't been out to their place since last winter when everything was white and cold and beautiful. But today it was green and lush and beautiful. And the lake was so blue it almost made your eyes hurt. "I can't believe I get to have my reception in such a fantastic location," I told her as she gave me a little tour of the grounds. "And look at those flowers." I pointed to the planters. "Is it just a coincidence that they're pale pink and white?"

She laughed. "I planted those annuals especially for you."

"Thank you!"

We finally decided where things would go. Tables and chairs down in the grass, the largest deck reserved for dancing, the other deck for refreshments. I even picked out some spots for photos. Like on the dock where we figure the sun will be setting not too long after we get there. "Will it be too dark out here at night?" I asked her.

"Don't worry," she assured me. "Your mom and aunt have that all figured out. Now, do you have time to come inside for a glass of iced tea?"

"That sounds lovely."

I noticed the gorgeous bouquet as soon as I got inside. "Those flowers are amazing."

She nodded. "They're from Josh's grandmother. Mrs. Brown was by here this weekend to talk with me about the flower arrangements, and she brought these."

"She came out here to talk about the flowers?" I was impressed.

"Yes, she wants to get them just right, and it was important for her to see the setting."

"Did she like it?"

Patty smiled as she handed me a tall glass of tea. "Yes. Shall we take these out on the deck?"

Once we were seated comfortably on the deck, I had to take in a deep breath and just sigh. "This place feels like a little bit of heaven to me."

Patty nodded, but I noticed the troubled look in her expression, and suddenly I remembered about Tom. Not that I'd forgotten, but with so much going on, and then planning for the reception...

"It's been good therapy for me," she said, "keeping busy and getting the place ready. I'm really thankful that you and Josh are letting us do this."

I kind of laughed. "Letting you? We can't believe what a gift this is to us."

"It's a gift to me too."

"Is it getting any better for you?" I asked, wondering if I even should. "I mean, I've heard that time heals all wounds, but I'm not sure if it's really true."

"I think it's partially true. But there are definitely some days when it's not. Some days I can hardly get up in the morning."

My heart ached for her.

"Some days all I can think of is what I would do just to be able to see his face again, to hug him and to tell him how much I love him."

Now I knew I was getting into touchy territory, and I didn't want to say anything to upset her, but I just couldn't say nothing. "I didn't really know Tom," I began slowly. "But I do know that he made a huge life decision while he was over in Iraq."

She studied me carefully then nodded. "Yes, Josh mentioned this shortly after Tom's death."

"As a result, I fully expect to see him again someday." I think I was praying silently just then, praying that I wouldn't offend or hurt her by this.

"I wish I had that kind of faith."

"You don't really have to have that kind of faith for yourself," I said.

"What do you mean?"

"I mean that God can give you that kind of faith, if you can just get to a place where you're ready to ask Him."

She nodded without speaking.

"He wants us to ask Him, Patty. He's just waiting to give us the faith that we so desperately need."

It was quiet for a bit, and she seemed to actually

consider my words, but then she changed the subject back to the reception, and I left it at that. It's not like I wanted to preach at her, but I do get the feeling that God is at work in her. I'll be praying for both her and Bob more than ever now.

Finally it was time to go, and I hugged and thanked her again for opening her home up like this for us.

DEAR GOD, PLEASE SHOW PATTY THAT YOU ALONE ARE THE GIVER OF FAITH. HELP HER TO TURN HER EYES TO YOU, HELP HER TO PLACE HER ACHING HEART IN YOUR HANDS, AND PLEASE BLESS HER IN A BIG WAY FOR HER GENEROSITY TO JOSH AND ME. AMEN.

Tuesday, May 30

Several months ago, I'd read in one of those brides' magazines that it's my responsibility to host a luncheon for the bridesmaids, as well as to give them gifts. And so I had scheduled it for today. My grandma helped me to fix a lunch of quiche and salad and several other good things, including strawberries dipped in chocolate—my personal favorite.

And I'd spent most of the day yesterday just straightening up her backyard, which had been pretty neglected this spring—as well as working on my tan, since Josh has informed me that we're going to someplace beachy for our honeymoon. I'm not sure if this means we'll be sleeping on some Mexican beach or not, but as long as I'm with Josh I won't worry.

I finally got her patio and flowerpots looking somewhat respectable, and I put a pretty tablecloth on the picnic table and set it with her good china. It really looked rather nice. At least Beanie, Jenny, and Chloe were impressed.

"You're becoming quite domestic," said Jenny approvingly.

"A real Martha Stewart," added Beanie.

"Yeah, yeah." I set the quiche in the center of the table. "Grandma coached me a lot."

But we had a good time just sitting in the sun, eating, and talking. And then Beanie offered to model a bridesmaid dress since I've yet to see the whole thing on anyone, and she still needed to try hers on.

"Hey, these aren't bad," she said when she came back outside wearing the pale pink gown and killer shoes. They are also pale pink with very high heels and look just like a Manolo Blahnik but at a fraction of the price. "I might not wear this dress again, but I think I could have some fun with these shoes."

"I was wondering about long white gloves with the dress," Jenny said as she stood and surveyed Beanie.

I considered this, then shook my head. "I think that would look overdone."

Beanie nodded. "I agree."

"Me too," said Chloe.

"But the outfit still needs something," I said as I

reached under the table for a bag I'd stowed there earlier. I pulled out a wrapped box for each of them and handed them around.

"These are gorgeous," said Jenny, the first one to get hers opened. "Tell me they're not for real!" She held a pearl necklace up to the sunlight and peered at them.

"I wish," I told her. "But not on my budget." However, and I didn't mention this, these cultured pearls were not cheap, and the teardrop earrings had fourteen carat gold posts on them. We helped Beanie put hers on, then all stepped back to look.

"Flowers," said Jenny. "That's what's missing."

"Right." Then I described the bouquets I'd ordered. "These are the only flowers that are costing anything," I told them. "Pale pink rosebuds for the bridesmaids and groomsmen, and white for Josh and me."

"Speaking of groomsmen," said Beanie. "Who is Josh having?"

Now I specifically hadn't mentioned this to Beanie yet. But I could see there was no more putting it off.

"Actually, I'm not totally sure."

"Huh?" Beanie peered at me.

"Well, I know that my brother Ben is one. And Zach."

"Zach?" Beanie frowned. "Are you serious?"

"Zach and Josh have been friends for a long time," I reminded her.

"Yeah, I know."

"Come on, Beanie," teased Jenny. "You still carrying a torch for that boy?"

Beanie shook her head. "Not even. But I guess it's kind of weird." Then she smiled. "At least maybe I'll have someone to dance with now."

"But who's the third guy?" asked Jenny.

"Josh won't tell me. He says because it's not totally for sure."

Then Beanie changed back into her regular clothes, and just when I thought it was probably time to wind this thing down (not that I wanted my friends to leave), the party suddenly switched gears. We were still out in the backyard when several of my other girlfriends suddenly appeared, and then Grandma came out with a cake that I hadn't even seen her making. And then my mom and Aunt Steph arrived, and I could tell that something was definitely going on here.

"What's up?" I asked Beanie since she seemed to be in the know.

"Just a little shower for the bride-to-be."

"But I already had one—"

"Not like this," she said with a wink. Jenny and Chloe were already setting out a circle of lawn chairs in the yard, and then Beanie took my hand and led me out there and told me to sit down. Before long, about a dozen of my closest female friends were all gathered around me. Even Liz was there! And Anna, fully pregnant now and looking as if she was ready to go into labor at any moment.

Of course, I should've known that this was a personal shower, but I'm sure my jaw dropped a couple of inches when the first present I opened (from Steph, even!) was a scanty black teddy from Victoria's Secret. I stood and held up the flimsy garment while my friends made appropriate hoots and comments.

"Wow, Aunt Steph," I finally said. "This is pretty steamy coming from a pastor's wife."

But she just laughed. "God's the one who invented sex, Caitlin. Who should enjoy it more than a pastor's wife?"

And so it went, one embarrassing garment after another. Oh, they weren't all as risqué as Aunt Steph's. Some were more practical, like Laura's gift of bath oil and lotion. And my mom even got me a coupon for a facial, pedicure, and manicure.

"I got it several weeks ago," she told me. "And I went ahead and made you an appointment for tomorrow morning if you're interested."

"Interested?" I said. "I can't wait!"

I finally opened the last gift, which happened to be from Liz. I was curious since it was in a fairly large box, but I just had to crack up when I pulled out a pair of pink footy pajamas.

"Thanks, Liz." I stood and held them up.

And as cool as anything she said, "I figured it was perfect for your wedding night. No sense in giving it all away just because you're married, right?"

Well, I didn't know what to say, but everyone else was kind of snickering.

"Oh, yeah, there's something else in the box that you

might want to wear under those."

So I dug around until I found some tissue wrapped around the scantiest bra and panties imaginable. They were pale pink and nothing but lace. I looked at Liz and nodded. "Okay, Liz, I get you." And everyone just laughed.

DEAR GOD, SUDDENLY I'M VERY AWARE OF THE "PHYSICAL UNION" THAT IN JUST TWO DAYS JOSH AND I WILL BE ENTERING INTO, AND I AM FEELING REALLY NERVOUS. PLEASE, HELP ME TO REMEMBER THAT WE'RE DOING THIS THING YOUR WAY AND THAT EVERYTHING SHOULD BE JUST FINE. AS IN ALL THINGS, I TRUST YOU WITH THIS TOO. AMEN.

Wednesday, May 31

After enjoying a couple of hours of sweet pampering (I have happy toes, hands, and face now), I came back to my grandma's house and got out a big fat novel I've been dying to read, and I laid out in the sun for about an hour, then had a nice long nap. Talk about a lazy day. And I don't feel the least bit guilty. In fact, it was Aunt Steph who insisted I do nothing today. "Nothing with a capital N," she said. And that's just what I did.

Then it was time to go to the church for our wedding rehearsal, and I was totally stunned to see that Josh's mysterious best man was actually his older brother, Caleb. Now, I'd never actually met Caleb, but I knew that he'd struggled with drug addiction and has been somewhat estranged from the family, although it's gotten better during this last year. But I never expected him to be in our wedding.

"I would've told you," Josh said when we were out of earshot, "but I was afraid you'd be worried. And until last week I wasn't even sure that he was really going to come through."

"He looks so good," I said. "I thought Chloe said he was kind of a mess."

"He got the haircut just for the wedding."

"That's sweet. How are your parents taking it?"

"Dad's shocked, but recovered. Mom's been crying a lot. And Chloe is ecstatic." He looked at me. "How are you with it? I mean, I realize that he's not saved and still has a lot of prob—"

"He's your brother, Josh," I said quickly. "And he's going to be my brother-in-law. And if you want him as your best man, that's good enough for me."

"We better get this thing going," called out Tony. "I hear they have another rehearsal in here at seven."

So we all took our places and ran through the paces a couple of times. Then we went back to the Miller house, where Joy had arranged for a catered meal for the entire wedding party. I could tell she was on needles and pins though, and I wanted to say something reassuring to her. But every time I got within a few feet, she scurried away. I almost began to take it personally, but Chloe pulled me aside and told me that her mom was walking a fine line emotionally just now.

"I think we all just need to give her some space," she quietly warned me. "But don't worry, I'm sure she'll be okay by tomorrow."

"Thanks, I'll be praying for her."

I guess it didn't really occur to me that weddings can be stressful on a lot of people. Maybe it's because I've been feeling pretty relaxed and laid-back today. But now I'm reminded that lots of feelings are involved, and gatherings like this tend to ignite memories. I suppose, in some ways, it's kind of like an emotional minefield.

DEAR GOD, I PRAY THAT YOUR PRESENCE WILL BE FELT BY EVERYONE AT OUR WEDDING AND RECEPTION TOMORROW. I PRAY THAT YOUR LOVE AND GRACE WILL BE FLOWING AND THAT STRESS WILL BE REDUCED TO A MINIMUM. AMEN.

TWENTY

Monday, June 5

Here I am sitting on a sunny beach in
Hawaii, just listening to the waves slapping the shore as
Josh makes another attempt at surfing. Yes, we are on
our honeymoon, and it's been totally amazing and wonderful.

But oh, you ask me, dear diary—<u>what about the
wedding?</u> Come on, I want to hear about the wedding?
Okay, let me get this down while it's still fresh in my
mind.

After a relatively quiet day (for me anyway; I'm not
sure about everyone else), I went over to my parents' house
and started getting my things together for the actual
ceremony. I'd already gotten my bags packed for the honeymoon (somewhere beachy was all I'd been told), and one
of Josh's youth group guys stopped by to pick up my stuff
(since Josh and I had decided to be old-fashioned and

not see each other until it was time for me to actually walk down the aisle).

I was back in my old room (which is really mom's craft room), but all the wedding decorations were long gone by now. Beanie came over later in the afternoon to help me with my hair and makeup—it's like she had this certain image she wanted to create that would go with the dress. And when she was done, I had to agree it was perfect. Fortunately, it was a fairly natural look (my favorite), and I didn't feel as if she'd turned me into someone else. Even my hair, though pulled up, still looked soft and natural. Very nice.

"Something old, something new, something borrowed, something blue," she was saying to me as my mom came into my room. "Do you have it covered?"

I held up the blue garter that Grandma had made for me. "And almost everything is new."

"And I loaned you my pearl barrette for your hair," Mom said. "But what about old?"

I shrugged. "How about me? I'm getting old just sitting here and waiting for this wedding to happen."

They laughed, then my mom looked at Beanie and she nodded. I could tell these two knew something I didn't.

"I know you were thinking about wearing pearls tonight..." began my mom. And this was true. I'd gotten myself a string of pearls just like the bridesmaids'. "But Beanie and I thought something else might look better." Then she held out an old necklace that has been in my mom's family for a long time. I hadn't seen it for a while and had nearly forgotten all about it. But as she held it in front of me, I could see it was absolutely perfect, and Beanie was nodding.

"I was going to wait until we were at the church." My mom fastened the lovely gold chain around my neck, then adjusted the pearl pendant in the center. "But I wanted to make sure you were okay—"

"Okay?" I said. "This is way better than okay."

"And way better than those pearls," said Beanie. "No offense, because I think they look fantastic with the bridesmaids' dresses, but they were just too heavy-looking for you. You needed something more delicate, and when your mom showed me this..." She sighed happily. "Well, it was perfect."

That's not all that was perfect. I will never forget the feeling when it was time for Dad to walk me down the aisle. First of all, he looked super and his smile was something that will be with me always, but when I got to the place where I could see the wedding party in front, well, I almost fainted. Thank God, I didn't. But it was so like that "wedding vision" I'd had last winter that for a moment I thought it wasn't real.

All the white candles were glowing, and the ivy and flowers were just the right touch, and there were my three best friends looking elegantly classy in their pale pink gowns. (And oh, those shoes!) And there were the groomsmen looking sophisticated and grown up. (Yes, even Ben, who is almost as tall as Josh now, and even Aunt

Steph's son little Oliver—now seven—standing so proudly as he held the pillow that held the rings.) And Josh's young cousin Elena in her pale pink dress and basket of rose petals that had been tossed along the aisle. It was all so perfect that I felt somewhat breathless and light-headed.

And then I locked eyes with Josh!

Okay, I know it's cliché, but my heart did skip a beat when I saw him. It wasn't so much because he was so handsome, but believe me, he was! He totally was! But it was the expression on his face that took my breath away as I slowly walked toward him. His eyes were so bright and his smile was so genuine that I knew, beyond any shadow of doubt, this man truly loved me. I knew that he would take good care of me. And I knew that he had been worth waiting for.

I think I was starting to cry then, which made this scene even more like my "wedding vision," because it got just slightly blurry. But then as Dad kissed me and placed my hand in Josh's, I took a deep breath and just focused on my true love's face.

No one does a wedding like Pastor Tony. He spoke from the heart and made it feel as if God was right there with us—and I know that He was. Not only that, but Pastor Tony doesn't go on too long. As we exchanged the rings, he reminded us that the circle of the ring was like the never-ending circle of God's love for us and our love for each other.

We both got a little teary eyed as we said our vows,

and the next thing I knew, we were kneeling for communion and Kim Peterson was playing the most beautiful violin solo of "Ave Maria." I even got goose bumps.

And suddenly Pastor Tony was pronouncing us "husband and wife," and we were kissing and being introduced to everyone as "Mr. and Mrs. Joshua Miller." Well, you should've heard the cheers.

The guests were excused to head out to the reception, and we'd been promised by the photographer (a college buddy of Josh's who was giving us a real deal) that the church photos would take less than twenty minutes. We made him stick to his promise, because we didn't want our guests to be waiting too long.

Then as we were heading out of the church, I spotted a white stretch limousine approaching, and I looked at Josh, thinking that couldn't possibly be for us—but it was. Josh was just as surprised as I was, but it turned out that Chloe had ordered it. All eight of us got in and were driven in style over to Patty and Bob's beautiful lakeside home.

Honestly, it just got better and better after that. The yard looked amazing with all the white-covered tables and flower arrangements. It wasn't long before the sun was going down on the lake, and there was just enough cloud in the sky to give everything a soft, rosy glow. "I think that's for you," Josh whispered in my ear. "A special wedding greeting."

The most money I'd spent on anything for the wedding was to have a catered buffet for the guests. It had just seemed the right thing to do, and I think every-one enjoyed it. I particularly enjoyed the strawberries dipped in chocolate that Aunt Steph had spent all last night making.

"You did this for me?" I said as I hugged her.

"I wouldn't do it for anyone else!"

The wedding cake was beautiful AND delicious. Even the band was good—and man, were they excited to meet Jeremy Baxter! Then Chloe, Allie, and Laura got up there and played a song that Chloe had written for Josh and me, called "Just Waiting." Of course, it made us both cry. And then to lighten the mood, she and the girls did a number that totally rocked the house.

As the evening shadows grew longer, I noticed dainty strings of white lights hanging in the trees and around deck railings. And I think little fairies went around light-ing about a hundred candles that were protected from the lake breeze by glass jars. It was truly magical.

Besides being with Josh, one of my favorite moments at the reception was when Joy came and took me aside. At first I was worried that something had gone wrong because her face looked somewhat serious.

"You've put together the most beautiful wedding ever," she told me. "And I want to apologize for all the grief I'm sure I put you through." She shook her head. "I just couldn't imagine how you could possibly pull this off. Especially when you seemed so unconcerned about everything."

I kind of laughed. "Oh, it's not that I wasn't concerned. It's just that I was really trying to trust God."

"Yes, that's the same thing Josh and Chloe keep telling me. But for some reason, you kids seem to understand these things better." She smiled. "I guess it's like they say, a child shall lead them." Then she gave me a big hug. "I am so proud to have you for my daughter-in-law, Caitlin. Josh is one lucky young man."

Well, I thought that was pretty good coming from her. And I did forgive her for all the times when she questioned me or made me feel like I was clueless when it came to weddings. The truth of the matter is, I actually was fairly naive. But I think I got the important things right. And that made all the difference.

One of the funniest moments (for me) was when Josh's second cousin Meg cornered me and demanded to know who my wedding planner was (she's getting married next year). I smiled at her and said, "God." She just looked at me like I hadn't heard her right, then repeated her question. "God," I said again. "The divine wedding planner." Then she shook her head and probably assumed I was suffering from wedding day overload.

Oh, there were lots of great moments at the reception. I'm sure they're all filed somewhere in my memory. But mostly I remember how Josh held on to my hand and how he kept looking into my eyes and reminding me that this was for real.

And finally, it was getting late, and I knew it was time to get ready to go. I went into Patty's elegant guest room to change into my "going away" outfit, selected by

Beanie and quite stylish as it turned out. But before I could leave, I just had to drop to my knees and thank God for all the miracles in my life—not just for this day—but all along the way.

Then I went back outside and was told that the bridesmaids wanted me to go stand on the dock to throw my wedding bouquet. So, hoping they didn't plan to toss me into the drink, I complied.

Standing on the dock, I turned my back to the young women who were gathered around, hoping to catch my beautiful roses (which I had already instructed Beanie to rescue afterward since I plan to save them), and I gave it a big underhand toss. And guess who caught it? Chloe Miller.

Well, I had to laugh at that, and I did remind her that she was way too young to even think about it. But she just grinned in typical Chloe fashion. Then she pointed over my shoulder and said, "Hey, looks like your getaway is here." Surprised, I turned to the lake to see a white motorboat approaching.

"Let's go, Caitie," Josh said as he grabbed my hand. And suddenly everyone was throwing birdseed (better than rice on the Miller's lovely grounds), and Josh and I were running to get into the boat.

Of course, his youth group boys were disappointed since they had some crazy chase planned. And I'd already seen the Jeep all covered in toilet paper, whipped cream, and tin cans. But I didn't mind avoiding that as Josh and I sat in the back of the boat and waved to our guests as we pulled out, leaving a wake behind us. Of course, we shared some nice kisses as we enjoyed a quick ride across the lake.

Then we were met by a taxi, ordered by Josh, and taken to the nicest hotel in our area. And here comes the part where even my diary doesn't get to hear about everything. But trust me, it was good.

It wasn't until the next morning that Josh told me where we were going on our honeymoon. I was preparing myself for the fleabag motel in Tijuana when he pulled a packet out of his jacket pocket. "Compliments of Chloe. She made me promise not to tell you until we were on our way."

And that's why I am sitting here on one of the most beautiful beaches in Maui right now. We have another whole week before we fly down to Mexico. Chloe booked the tickets so that we could go directly to the mission. And Josh arranged for a couple of college guys to drive his Jeep down, so we'll have it to use and drive back when we're done.

"Do you think God will keep us in Mexico longer than just for the summer?" I asked my sweet husband this morning.

He got a slightly puzzled look just then. "I'm not sure. I've always been open to staying down there indefinitely. And I still am. But I have to admit that as we were getting things ready for the wedding, and then even at the wedding, it occurred to me how many friends and family members we have that still need God's touch in their lives. And then there's the youth group."

"Yeah, I know."

"So, what are you thinking?" he asked.

"I guess I'm open to wherever God wants to take us."

He grinned. "That's what I love about you, Caitlin."

And that's what I love about him too. I know that, more than anything, we both want to serve God with our whole hearts. And wherever that takes us and however we get there, it'll all be worth it in the end.

The End

(Or beginning...)

Discussion Questions

1. What did you think about Josh asking Caitlin's dad if he could marry her? How would you feel if you were in Caitlin's shoes?

2. What do you think Caitlin loves most about Josh? Why?

3. What qualities would you look for in a husband? List ten.

4. Why do you think Caitlin didn't want to spend a fortune on her wedding? Do you think she was just being cheap? How much do you think a wedding should cost?

5. Why do you think Caitlin struggled so hard with the fact that Josh had slept with Jenny? How would you feel in the same situation?

6. How do you think Josh felt about the fact that he, unlike Caitlin, wasn't a virgin?

7. Families tend to get very involved in weddings. Do you think the wedding should be more about families, or more about the couple? Why?

8. Which is more important—the wedding or the marriage? Which do engaged couples usually focus on more—the wedding or the marriage? Why?

9. What do you think was the most memorable part of Caitlin's wedding day? What would you want to be most memorable if you were the one getting married?

10. Why did the details for Caitlin's wedding seem to fall so perfectly into place? A trick of fiction? Or the result of someone trusting God completely? [Hint: The author's wedding wasn't so unlike Caitlin's.]

Sneak a peek inside the head of Chloe's friend Kim Peterson as she deals with all the stuff teens face...like feeling different. Kim's used to standing out. She's Asian. She's adopted. She's a good student and a talented musician. But now Kim has a new job that *won't* make her stand out—she's an anonymous teen advice columnist for the local paper! But there's one question Kim's not finding easy answers for...just what *is* God all about?

Don't miss Kim's first diary—*Just Ask*—coming August 2005!

AUGUST 30

I never would've guessed that my own father would resort to using blackmail against me. I mean, I'm his only daughter, his "little princess." But it seems Dad has sunk to new depths lately.

I suppose it's just the desperate cry of a frustrated newspaperman who lives in a rather small and boring town, where big news only happens once in a great while. Like the time that guy went bonkers and shot a bunch of kids at McFadden High. I was still in middle school then, but the whole town was turned inside out over the tragedy.

Dad ran stories in his paper for weeks, some that were even picked up by national news services. He actually keeps those articles framed and hanging above his desk, which I personally think is kind of flaky. But I don't let on.

Now it's not like we want these disasters (like the McFadden shooting) to happen on a regular basis, but as my dad says, "That's what sells papers."

Of course, we have other kinds of news too. Our local paper has recently enjoyed the celebrity of the Christian rock band Redemption. Which is one of the reasons my dad started a new section in the paper called "Teen Beat." The title is a pretty lame name, if you ask me, although he didn't. Anyway, I make an extra effort to keep him informed of Redemption's latest news (like when they won that award last spring). I do this because Chloe Miller is a good friend and has been for years, not just after she became rich and famous. Some user-types of people really take advantage of her generous nature, and what's weird is that she actually lets them. She says it's because she's a Christian, and that just makes me scratch my head and go, "Huh?" Still, I really like and respect Chloe, and despite her whole Christianity thing, she seems like a genuine person. And even though she knows that I'm not so sure about the whole religion thing, Chloe still treats me like I'm a decent human being.

Oh, it's not like I'm a "perfect heathen," as my mom likes to tease when I skip out on church. I used to go pretty regularly with my parents (well, only because they made me), and I'm sure it's just fine for some people, but it's not for me. Fortunately I was able to avoid church a lot this past summer due to my job at the mall, which I recently had to quit because school just started and my parents felt it would be "too distracting" to my education. Yeah, sure!

Back to my dad and how he's blackmailing his only daughter. You see, I got my driver's license last year and have been saving for my own car ever since. My parents told me that they would match what I'd saved when I was ready to buy one. And I was almost ready. But then my parents cooked up this little deal. Mostly it's my mom's idea, since she's totally freaked that I'm going to drive recklessly and get myself killed.

Anyway, they decided I can only get a car if I keep a clean driving record. That means NO tickets. Well, I was driving my mom's car to work yesterday. And her car's just a frumpy 1998 Buick LeSabre (not exactly a race car, if you know what I mean). It was my last day of work, I'd forgotten to set my alarm, and I was running a little late. So you can imagine my surprise when I heard that wailing siren and saw those flashing blue lights in my rearview mirror. Now, if I'd been a praying kind of person, I would've begged God to spare me from getting a speeding ticket, but as you already know, I am not. The policeman said he'd clocked me going seventy-two in a fifty-five zone.

"You were going seventeen miles an hour over the

limit, young lady," he told me, like he thought I was unable to do simple math. And I was the mental math champion throughout grade school, until I realized it wasn't so cool to appear that smart on a regular basis.

"But everyone drives sixty-five through here. So it's more like I was only going seven miles over the limit." I guess I actually hoped he'd change the ticket or something.

But this man had no mercy for speeding teenage girls. "The law's the law." He handed me the ticket. "You'd better slow down before you get hurt."

When I looked down at the ticket, I actually cried. Not just because it was for $285, but also because I knew this would mean no car.

After work, I went to my dad's newspaper office. "Daddy," I began in my sweetest little princess voice. "I have something to tell you, and I don't want you to get mad. Okay?"

I could tell by his expression that he was expecting the worst. Like what would that be? Did he think I was pregnant or had a bad coke-snorting habit or was wanted by the FBI? Anyway, I told him my sad story, making it as pitiful as possible. But I could sense his relief that it wasn't something way more serious.

"I'm really sorry, Daddy. And I promise I won't speed again. I'm sure I've learned my lesson, and I plan to pay the whole fine myself." Now I managed to actually work up a few tears. (I'm in drama and love putting on a good show.) "I just don't know what I'll do if I can't get my own car now. I can't bear to ride the school bus, Daddy. I mean, think how stupid I'll look. I'm a junior this year. Only a geeky junior would ride the school bus." And then when he looked unconvinced, I told him some horror stories about what happens to geeky kids who ride the bus.

"Oh, Kim, I think you're exaggerating."

So I put on my best pouty face and pulled out my final trump card. "Sometimes I get teased for being...well...you know...different."

Now this isn't completely untrue. Being the adopted Korean child of your basic all-American white-bread Caucasian parents truly does mean that sometimes I'm treated differently. I was adopted as an infant, and occasionally I can make it really work for me. And I have to admit I was working it then.

"Oh, honey." My dad sighed and shook his head, and I wasn't sure if he felt bad or was seeing right through me. After all, he is a managing editor and is pretty good at sniffing out the truth.

"Really, Daddy. The kids on the bus can be so mean. Sometimes they even call me names." And then I actually repeated a couple of slang words that my dad cannot stand to hear. And I knew I almost had him where I wanted him.

He got this thoughtful expression as he drummed his pencil up and down like a skinny woodpecker pecking on the rim of his coffee cup. Then he pressed his lips tightly together in that I-am-getting-an-idea sort of look. And that started to scare me.

Finally, he spoke up. "Okay, Kim, how about this?"
Then he paused to study me for what felt like a full
minute before he continued. "How about if we keep this
one ticket between you and me?"

"Really?" I could hardly believe my good fortune. This
was way easier than I'd expected.

He nodded. "But only if you agree to do something in
return."

"Huh?"

"I want you to write the advice column for Teen Beat."

"Oh, Daddy!" I frowned as I sunk into the chair across
from his desk. My dad had been pestering me all summer
to do this stupid column for him. He honestly thought
that teens would write letters to his newspaper—just like
"Dear Abby"—and that they would actually read the
answers that some lame person (hopefully, not me!) wrote
back in response.

"Come on, Kim. We're making a deal here. Are you in
or not?"

I slouched lower into the chair, and folding my arms
across my chest, I decided to try my pouting routine again.

But he wasn't falling for it this time. "You're a good
writer, sweetheart. And you've got a good head on your
shoulders. Plus you're very mature for your age. Honestly,
I really think you can do this."

"But I don't want to do this." I sat up straight and
looked him right in the eyes. "Don't you understand how
stupid I'd look? I don't want kids going around school say-

ing, 'Kim Peterson writes that lame advice column in Teen Beat. Like who does she think she is anyway?'"

He held up his hands to stop me. "No, no, you don't understand. No one will ever know that you're the writer. You have to remain anonymous for it to work. We'll give you a pseudonym or something."

"Really?"

"Of course."

"And you wouldn't tell Mom about my speeding ticket?"

"It'll be part of our deal. You don't tell anyone you're writing this column for me, and I won't tell Mom that you got the ticket."

"And I can still get a car?"

He nodded. "You'll even get paid."

"I'll get paid?"

He shrugged. "Well, not much, honey. But we'll work out something."

And so that's how I got stuck with this small pile of letters (supposedly from teens) for "Just Ask Jamie"— that's the actual name of the advice column. Of course, Dad didn't just ask if I wanted it called that. But I guess it's okay. Although I wish he'd come up with something better for my pseudonym than Jamie. But he said he wanted to use a unisex name so that kids wouldn't know whether I was a guy or a girl. Whatever. Also, my dad's linked me up with some "resources" for any tricky questions that may involve the law or anything that's outside of my expertise. "Like what exactly is my expertise?" I asked him. And he just laughed and assured me that I would be fine. We'll see.

Anyway, I've just finished practicing violin (I have to get back into shape before school starts), and I decided I would "practice write" my answers to these letters in the safety zone of my own computer diary (which is accessible only with my secret password). I figure this will help me to see how it goes and whether I can really pull this thing off or not.

I've picked the first letter that I plan to answer. Mostly, I picked this one because it's a fairly simple and straightforward question. So here goes nothing.

Dear Jamie,
I am fifteen years old, and I desperately want to get my belly button pierced. My mom says, "Not as long as you're living under my roof!" But I say, "Hey, it's my belly button, and it should be up to me if I want to put a hole in it or not." Right? Anyway, I plan to get it done soon. And I've decided not to tell my mom. Do you think I'm wrong to secretly do this?
Holeyer than Some

Dear Holeyer,
While I can totally understand wanting to pierce your belly button because I, too, happen to think that looks pretty cool when done right, I really think you should consider some things first. Like how is your mom going

*to feel when she finds out you did this behind her back?
Because they always find out. And how will this mess
up your relationship with her? Whether you like it or
not, you'll probably be stuck living "under her roof" for
about three more years. So why not try to talk this thing
through with her? Explain that you could go behind her
back, but that you'd rather have her permission. Believe
me, you'll enjoy your pierced belly button a whole lot
more if you don't pierce your mom's heart along with it.
Just Jamie*

Okay, now I have a problem. I feel like a total hypocrite because I haven't been completely honest with my
mom. Oh, sure, I didn't go out and pierce my belly button. Although that might not be as bad as breaking the
law, getting a ticket, and then not telling her. Of course,
my dad did make a deal with me when he blackmailed me
with the advice column. So maybe this is different. But if
this is different, why do I feel guilty? Maybe I should write
a letter to Jamie and just ask!

THE DIARY OF A TEENAGE GIRL SERIES

ENTER CAITLIN'S WORLD

DIARY OF A TEENAGE GIRL, Caitlin book one

Follow sixteen-year-old Caitlin O'Conner as she makes her way through life—surviving a challenging home life, school pressures, an identity crisis, and the uncertainties of "true love." You'll cry with Caitlin as she experiences heartache, and cheer for her as she encounters a new reality in her life: God. See how rejection by one group can—incredibly—sometimes lead you to discover who you really are.

ISBN 978-1-57673-735-4

IT'S MY LIFE, Caitlin book two

Caitlin faces new trials as she strives to maintain the recent commitments she's made to God. Torn between new spiritual directions and loyalty to Beanie, her pregnant best friend, Caitlin searches out her personal values on friendship, dating, life goals, and family.

ISBN 978-1-59052-053-6

WHO I AM, Caitlin book three

As a high school senior, Caitlin's relationship with Josh takes on a serious tone via e-mail—threatening her commitment to "kiss dating goodbye." When Beanie begins dating an African-American, Caitlin's concern over dating seems to be misread as racism. One thing is obvious: God is at work through this dynamic girl in very real but puzzling ways, and a soul-stretching time of racial reconciliation at school and within her church helps her discover God's will as never before.

ISBN 978-1-59052-890-0

ON MY OWN, Caitlin book four

An avalanche of emotion hits Caitlin as she lands at college and begins to realize she's not in high school anymore. Buried in coursework and far from her best friend, Beanie, Caitlin must cope with her new roommate's bad attitude, manic music, and sleazy social life. Should she have chosen a Bible college like Josh? Maybe...but how to survive the year ahead is the big question right now!

ISBN 978-1-59052-017-8

THE DIARY OF A TEENAGE GIRL SERIES

ENTER CHLOE'S WORLD

MY NAME IS CHLOE, Chloe book one

Chloe Miller, Josh's younger sister, is a free spirit with dramatic clothes and hair. She struggles with her own identity, classmates, parents, boys, and—whether or not God is for real. But this unconventional high school freshman definitely doesn't hold back when she meets Him in a big, personal way. Chloe expresses God's love and grace through the girl band she forms, Redemption, and continues to show the world she's not willing to conform to anyone else's image of who or what she should be. Except God's, that is.

ISBN 978-1-59052-018-5

SOLD OUT, Chloe book two

Chloe and her fellow band members must sort out their lives as they become a hit in the local community. And after a talent scout from Nashville discovers the trio, all too soon their explosive musical ministry begins to encounter conflicts with family, so-called friends, and school. Exhilarated yet frustrated, Chloe puts her dream in God's hand and prays for Him to work out the details.

ISBN 978-1-59052-141-0

ROAD TRIP, Chloe book three

After signing with a major record company, Redemption's dreams are coming true. Chloe, Allie, and Laura begin their concert tour with the good-looking guys in the band Iron Cross. But as soon as the glitz and glamour wear off, the girls find life on the road a little overwhelming. Even rock solid Laura appears to be feeling the stress—and Chloe isn't quite sure how to confront her about the growing signs of drug addiction...

ISBN 978-1-59052-142-7

FACE THE MUSIC, Chloe book four

Redemption has made it to the bestseller chart, but what Chloe and the girls need most is some downtime to sift through the usual high school stress with grades, friends, guys, and the prom. Chloe struggles to recover from a serious crush on the band leader of Iron Cross. Then just as an unexpected romance catches Redemption by surprise, Caitlin O'Conner—whose relationship with Josh is taking on a new dimension—joins the tour as their chaperone. Chloe's wild ride only speeds up, and this one-of-a-kind musician faces the fact that life may never be normal again.

ISBN 978-1-59052-241-7

ALSO FROM MELODY CARLSON

Dark Blue: Color Me Lonely
Brutally ditched by her best friend, Kara feels totally
abandoned until she discovers these dark blue days
contain a life-changing secret. 978-1-57683-529-6

Deep Green: Color Me Jealous
Stuck in a twisted love triangle, Jordan feels
absolutely green with envy until her former best friend,
Kara, introduces her to someone even more important
than Timothy. 978-1-57683-530-2

Torch Red: Color Me Torn
Zoë feels like the only virgin on Earth. But now that
she's dating Justin Clark, that seems like it's about to
change. Luckily, Zoë's friend Nate is there to try to
save her from the biggest mistake of her life.
978-1-57683-531-9

Pitch Black: Color Me Lost
Following her friend's suicide, Morgan questions the
meaning of life and death and God. As she struggles
with her grief, Morgan must make her life's ultimate
decision—before it's too late. 978-1-57683-532-6

Burnt Orange: Color Me Wasted
Amber Conrad has a problem. Her youth group friends
Simi and Lisa won't get off her case about the drinking
parties she's been going to. *Everyone does it. What's the
big deal?* Will she be honest with herself and her friends
before things really get out of control? 978-1-57683-533-3

Look for the TRUECOLORS series at a Christian bookstore
near you or order online at www.navpress.com.

truecolors

THINK

HEY, GOD, WHAT DO YOU WANT FROM ME?

More and more teens find themselves growing up in a world lacking in godly wisdom and direction. In *Piercing Proverbs,* bestselling youth fiction author Melody Carlson offers solid messages of the Bible in a version that can compete with TV, movies, and the Internet for the attention of this vital group in God's kingdom. Choosing life-impacting portions of teen-applicable Proverbs, Carlson paraphrases them into understandable, teen-friendly language and presents them as guidelines for clearly identified areas of life (such as friendship, family, money, and mistakes). Teens will easily read and digest these high-impact passages of the Bible delivered in their own words.

ISBN 978-1-57673-895-5